THE MYSTERY OF RUBY'S ROULETTE

ROSE DONOVAN

MOON SNAIL PRESS

MORE RUBY DOVE MYSTERIES

Join my reader group! Details can be found at the end of *The Mystery of Ruby's Roulette.*

Cast of Characters at Hotel Mansão Estoril

Ruby Dove – Student of chemistry at Oxford, fashion designer and amateur spy-sleuth. Posing as a Cape Verdean student in Estoril.

Fina Aubrey-Havelock – Student of history at Oxford, assistant seamstress to Ruby and her best friend. Posing as a student with a rich uncle.

Gayatri Badarur – Student of medicine at Oxford, friend to Ruby and Fina, with an affinity for gambling and sarcasm.

Pixley Hayford – A shameless journalist on the hunt for a scoop. Always game for a Ruby-and-Fina adventure.

Idris Maghur – Exiled architect from Tripoli with a love of history. And perhaps a love of someone else.

Doutor Fausto Tavares – Cape Verdean mathematician and linguist.

Elke Vogel – Dutch photographer with impeccable taste. Hendrik's wife.

Hendrik Vogel – Dutch importer-exporter of Zuster Chocolate. Elke's husband.

Jeremy Salter – Restless pilot from Cornwall.

Iveta Da Silva - Brazilian jeweller with an oversized personality to match her oversized gems.

Makeda Da Silva – Daughter of Iveta.

Princess Thalia – Princess of Denmark and Greece, wife of Charles II of Romania.

Florence Armitage – A sharp-tongued companion to the Princess.

Lena Fieraru – Romanian mistress of Charles II. A woman with definite personality.

Paulo Mariz – Manager of Hotel Mansão and the nearby casino. Owner of perfumery. A man with many financial interests.

Salvador Carvalho – Historian from Goa.

Teodoro Rapozo – Handsome croupier at the Hotel Mansão casino.

Comissário Cardoso – An elegant detective with a certain resemblance to the fabled Inspector Alleyn.

Cici – Lena's highly opinionated dog.

1

The door to Cabin 9 slammed shut in her face.

"Well, of all the rude…" Fina crossed her arms and blew a puff of air, lifting her fringe. Steadying herself against the rocking of the ship, she turned round to find her best friend, Ruby, dressed in an impeccably pressed navy frock.

Ruby smirked. "You realise why she shut the door, don't you?"

"All I know is that it was unforgivably rude."

"It's Princess Thalia's quarters. That's why her companion or maid shut the door."

Suitably impressed, Fina gulped but kept her arms crossed. "But all I wanted was to borrow a cigarette. And the door was ajar."

Now it was Ruby's turn to look surprised. "But you don't smoke!"

"It was for Pixley, you goose. He actually exhausted his seemingly never-ending supply of tobacco." Fina dashed towards the ship's bronze railing. Towards the blue of the Atlantic. "He was just here. Where did he disappear to?"

Ruby leaned over the railing and stared down at the white crest of the wake. "He must have realised we're going to dock soon – perhaps he went to pack."

"But Gayatri was with him. She's vanished, too."

"I'm sure they're in their cabins. We're all packed, so let's go distract them from their tasks." Ruby set off towards the bow of the ship.

Fina sucked in the sea air and smiled, despite the queasiness in her stomach. Off to their left, towards Lisbon, what must be the famous tower of Belém greeted them as a gateway to a magical place. Ruby pointed to it in the distance and waved.

Crowds of people queued on the ship's deck, also waving towards the shore. An occasional figure waved back, with one hand lifted from a fishing rod.

Ruby knocked on Pixley's blue-and-white door, adorned with the image of a cheerful whale.

Silence.

Despite the bile rising in her throat, Fina yelled, "Pixley!"

Gayatri's cabin was next door. They had the same disappointing result.

Ruby shrugged. "If we gather our suitcases, I'm sure we'll find them somewhere near the exit. Maybe one of them suddenly became seasick. Or ill."

But as they passed by the throng of chattering passengers, screaming children, and mountains of suitcases near the exit, Pixley and Gayatri were nowhere to be seen.

Back in their shared cabin, Ruby put a hand on Fina's shoulder. "Don't worry, Feens. They can't have vanished. We're all on a ship, remember?"

Fina gave her friend a rueful smile. "I'm certain you're right. But I can sense it. Something is, well, looming."

"What do you mean, 'looming'?" Ruby asked as they scanned the room for anything they might have missed.

Fina scooped up her suitcase and marched onto the deck. "It's that sense I get. You know. Atmosphere. Like a veil descending. Of evil."

The trumpet sleeves of Ruby's frock rippled. It was late December but the temperature was still mild as they sailed along the Tagus river. "Possibly. I don't doubt you. But it might be for any reason – on a ship with this many passengers, one can expect a few miscreants wandering about."

Fina nodded, despite her doubts. As she surveyed the crowd, half hoping the evildoer or evildoers would pop up and identify themselves, she spotted a petite figure with lustrous brown plaited hair.

"Gayatri! Thank goodness we've found you!"

Fina ran up to the woman and tapped her on the shoulder.

The head that turned round did not belong to Gayatri.

"Terribly sorry. Please do forgive me – I mistook you for someone else." The woman smiled and turned back towards a small child, who proceeded to wipe his lolly on her frock.

Ruby and Fina gripped the railings as the ship gently came to a halt. The white-uniformed crew lowered a gangplank and the crowd around the exit parted like the red sea as a steward began to shout. "Please, ladies and gentlemen. *Com licença!* We request you move away. Thank you!"

The crew held back the crowd as the woman who had shut the door in Fina's face now stepped onto the green rug that had been laid down towards the exit. She wore a little red lacquer hat, fashionably askew on her head. Her plain white trouser suit unfortunately created a washed-out, straw-like effect on her pale white skin. Behind her, a regal personage emerged, taking one step, then halting, then taking another.

Ruby leaned over and whispered, "That's Princess Thalia of Greece and Denmark. She's married to Charles II of Romania. I don't know how they managed to hide her this entire trip – her companion must be a marvel."

Princess Thalia, resplendent in an opal rose suit and a matching Florentine hat, floated down the green rug laid out for her. Nose held high, she nodded mechanically at the throngs of passengers, as if they were assembled for this royal sighting. Soon she and her companion, along with a coterie of various servants, were swallowed up by the crowd.

Ruby lifted her suitcase. "Do you have your passport? And do you remember your story?"

"But we're not going to repeat our stories to passport officials, are we?"

"Good point. I'm getting a little carried away by it all. Must be my nervousness about missing Pixley and Gayatri."

Fina studied Ruby. It wasn't often that her friend, who regularly took on high-society matrons in her fashion design business and miscreants in her sleuthing, admitted to nerves. Now, despite her words, not a line of worry creased her face. "But you're so calm, Ruby. Are you really nervous?"

Ruby bit her lip. "I am. I suspect it's also because it's your boyfriend who invited us on this spying adventure."

Fina stamped her foot. "Idris is not my boyfriend." Even as she uttered the words, she knew she sounded like a five-year-old child denying she's eaten four biscuits already. She could only hope Ruby had forgotten the way she'd blushed when the telegram from Idris had arrived, inviting them to meet him in Lisbon. "And we're not spying."

Ruby threw back her head and laughed. Wiping her eyes with her grandmother's blue handkerchief, she said, "Thanks, Feens. I needed a good laugh."

With a lump in her throat, Fina changed the subject. "Let's review our stories, shall we? It might be particularly important now that Gayatri and Pixley have vanished."

Ruby nodded. "I am a student at Oxford with Cape Verdean family. I forgot to tell you it's only a half-mistruth because we believe my mother's side of the family emigrated from Cape Verde to St Kitts fifty years ago. We don't know when my father's side arrived in St Kitts."

"Did Pixley ever decide on what story he was going to use for his cover?" Fina bounced on her toes, scanning the crowd – a fruitless gesture as she could barely see between people's heads.

"He told me he planned not to use a cover story. In other words, he'd use the truth. Easy for him – as a journalist, his stories sound wildly implausible no matter what. Instead of pretending to write a story about how Estoril is the most popular place in Europe for the rich and famous to congregate, he decided to try the truth."

"You mean the story about the Spanish official dying in a mysterious aeroplane crash as he flew from Estoril to Madrid?"

"Precisely. And Gayatri doesn't need a cover story, either. An Indian princess reading medicine at Oxford is certainly enough."

Fina tapped her passport against her cheek. "Yes. As for my story, I'm also a student at Oxford. And a good friend of yours. All of which is true. I have a rich uncle who sent me to spend early January – before Hilary Term begins – in a warmer climate. I have a rare illness, which means I need to spend time away from cold weather as much as possible. None of which is true. Especially the part about the uncle who gives me money!"

"Speaking of money, did your boyfriend – excuse me, Idris, or shall I say Mr Maghur – give us additional funds to travel to Estoril? It's more than an hour via car."

"But of course he did." Fina did her best to nonchalantly glance in her handbag while that familiar warmth crept up her neck.

All thoughts of Idris vanished, however, as she focused more intently on the bag. Scrabbling around, she shook her bag and finally stuck her head almost all the way inside. A panicked grunt ensued.

"Feens, what is it?"

"Ah. Ruby. My money seems to have vanished."

2

Ruby's mouth hung open. "Vanished? Let me have a look." She also poked her head inside the capacious handbag. But she came up empty-handed.

Groaning, Ruby pulled out her own small coin purse. "Nothing. All my Portuguese escudos have disappeared. Perhaps a pickpocket was on board and stole from both of us."

The rapidly dwindling passport control queue soon brought them face-to-face with a surly-looking man. Fina's stomach flipped as she noticed the tufts of grey hair sprouting from his cauliflower ears.

"Passport, *por favor.*"

Fina slid her passport across the desk. She looked at Ruby.

"*Seu passaporte, por favor.* Passport." The cauliflower-eared man drummed his fingers on the table.

In a frenzy, Ruby tipped over her handbag onto the table-top. Unlike Fina's bag, which was awash with detritus, Ruby's held self-contained smaller pouches and bags. She and Fina searched them, one by one.

Ruby slapped her hand on the table. "That's it. I gave it to Gayatri for safekeeping. She's so responsible."

"So are you! More responsible than I'll ever be."

A young man in a customs uniform tapped Ruby on the shoulder. "Please come with me."

"Wait!" Fina gripped the officer's arm. She dropped it, however, as soon as he gave her a backward-looking snarl.

The officer piloted Ruby into a small back office. Fina experienced a door slamming in her face for the second time that day. She pressed her face against the glass panel. The officer pulled down a window shade.

Fina turned away and hugged her handbag. After letting tears of frustration flow for a few minutes, she pulled herself together. She would repair her make-up in the lavatory and then decide what to do.

As she made her way past the table with the horrible cauliflower-eared man, she noticed he was embroiled in yet another confrontation.

Two people she had seen on the ship stood leaning over the desk. The woman, clad in glamorous wide-leg red trousers and navy blouse – complete with a splendidly slouching fedora – slammed her fist on the table. "Idiot! We are travellers of the world. Do you not understand?" Her spoken English was clipped – perhaps her first language was Dutch or German?

Her companion, who shared the same high aquiline nose and almost translucent white complexion, put a calming hand on the woman's arm and stared at the officer. "I am an importer-exporter. *Ja.* You understand chocolate?"

He turned to his companion and muttered under his breath, "I'm tired of this business."

The officer's jaw relaxed. "Chocolate?" He nodded eagerly. The officer's tendency towards *embonpoint* hinted he was a chocolate lover like Fina herself.

The man, who wore a chocolate-coloured suit, offered the

officer what appeared to be a tin of chocolate. "Zuster. You like Zuster, yes?"

The officer took the tin, examined it and put it in a drawer. He nodded at another officer behind him, who escorted the pair into a dingy back office.

Fina shook herself – she couldn't be distracted by such frivolities. But she must use the lavatory.

As she walked out of the impeccably clean bathroom, she squealed, "Gayatri! We've been looking for you everywhere!" She flung her arms around her friend as if they hadn't seen each other in years. "But Ruby has been detained! Where is Pixley?"

Despite the creases of worry around her eyes, Gayatri's glossy dark brown hair, secured in a long plait, glowed with good health.

Gayatri held the back of her hand against Fina's forehead. "You look feverish. Are you feeling ill?"

Resisting the urge to fling Gayatri's hand away from her forehead, Fina allowed it to remain, feeling slightly ridiculous. After all, Gayatri was a medical student. Must let her play doctor. "I'm sure my face is flushed – when is it not? It's just because I've been dashing about as blind as a hen in the night searching for you and Pixley, not to mention worrying about Ruby."

Gayatri moved her hand and squeezed Fina's upper arm. "What's happened to Ruby?"

"As I said, she's been detained by the authorities. She lost her passport. Where's Pixley?"

A dapper, stocky man in a white suit rushed towards them. He had pulled his hat down over his eyes against a light breeze. Fina didn't need to see his face, framed by owlish spectacles, to know it was Pixley Hayford – journalist, darling friend, fellow sleuth, and the proverbial life of the party.

"Feens! We'd given up on you. Weren't we supposed to meet in the library on the ship? Where's Ruby?"

WITHIN AN HOUR, all had been resolved. In her usual diplomatic fashion, Gayatri liberated Ruby from the customs officials. Fina still didn't know what had happened to her money, but the important point was they were all safe and en route to Estoril.

Every time their car bounced over the paving stones, Fina felt like she was still on the ship. She opened the window a crack and breathed in the smells of bread and grilled fish. As they whizzed past the ancient maze of the Alfama neighbourhood, filled with children's laughter and the mumbling of their mothers, she hoped they would have time to spend in Lisbon. Fina, like her friends, preferred simple pleasures to the luxury awaiting them at Estoril. Not that she would complain about a free ticket to a seaside resort and casino. And seeing Idris again...

Gayatri turned around from the front seat. Ruby had convinced her to wear a sea-foam green frock, which suited her much better than her usual brown crêpe. The dark circles under her eyes – a permanent fixture when they were at Oxford – had nearly disappeared. As soon as they'd set foot on the ship, away from their cares at Oxford, Gayatri's sarcastic streak had grown more pronounced and playful – a sure sign of happiness. "What are our instructions, intrepid Fina?"

"Idris said we'd have further instructions once we reached Hotel Mansão."

The driver coughed. His hands flew up in response to a child darting through the traffic.

"You received no further instructions?" asked Gayatri.

"I received a wire when we docked in Cherbourg for the day."

Ruby turned her face from the window. "And you didn't tell me?"

"Oh, I, ah..."

Pixley giggled. "It's because it's from her main squeeze, as they say in America."

The driver's hands flew up again, like delicate birds, as they halted. A few horns honked as they navigated through traffic.

"No, it's not that." Fina's voice rose as she became more defensive. "It's because it seemed rather mundane." It was a good time to read the wire aloud. She'd leave out the bit about being glad to see her.

Fina cleared her throat. "Will meet the four of you at Hotel Mansão on December 30th. Hire a driver at the port to take you to the hotel. Come in festive costume."

Pixley leaned over Fina's hand and wiggled his spectacles. "Love, Idris." He laughed and laughed.

"It does not say that. It says he's looking forward to seeing me."

"Stop teasing her, Pixley," Gayatri said, even as she had a twinkle in her eye.

The driver coughed again. He adjusted his rear-view mirror.

"Should you discuss such secrets out loud?" he asked.

That voice... Fina looked in the mirror. A tanned face with high cheekbones and amused eyes stared back.

"Idris!" Pixley, Fina, and Ruby exclaimed all at the same time. Fina hadn't noticed the driver when she slid into the back seat. Gayatri, who had not been with the trio on their Sardinian adventure, where they had all first met Idris, had no way of knowing what he looked like.

Still caught in traffic, Idris turned around and gave them a quick smile. Fina jumped forward and pecked him on the cheek, while Ruby clapped. Idris grinned even more broadly, causing the corners of his eyes to crinkle with pleasure.

Pixley held up a hand as Idris opened his mouth. "Lesson

learned. We should not discuss such things, especially on the assumption the driver only speaks Portuguese."

The cars in front of them began to move.

"Can you tell us more?"

"Yes, yes. I will explain soon. Once we arrive in Estoril, I'm afraid I will need to leave you all alone for a while as I have a great deal to attend to."

"You mean with other architects?" Fina asked.

"Ah, well – no. I told you I was an architect, and I am. It wasn't a lie. And it's true I'm Berber and Jewish. In exile from Libya. But, like you, and your friends, I'm involved in a campaign – a cause, shall we say. Since we're working towards the same goal, I decided to invite you all here."

"What, or who, are you posing as?"

Idris was on the point of answering when, without warning, he clamped his hands on the wheel. The car jerked. "Hold on!" he cried.

Fina barely had time to clutch the seat in front of her before the car took a violent swerve to the right.

3

"Ow!" Pixley rubbed his head.

Idris yanked the wheel again to the right, causing a screeching noise as he did so. Fina squeezed her eyes shut as a cat sauntered across the cobblestone road. The car swerved again, just missing the cat.

"What's happening?" cried Fina.

Pixley craned his neck behind him and peered through the window.

"We're being followed. By a grey motor-car."

"What kind of car?" Fina tried to squeeze her head near enough to Pixley to peep through the back window. No such luck.

"How should I know? Looks expensive, though."

"Who's the driver?"

"Their cap hides their face."

The car turned left, sending up a flurry of squawking chickens. As the road narrowed, the number of bumps increased. They pressed on, up a hill cresting at a small village.

"Are they still following us?" Idris slowed around a sharp

curve that would reward speed with a beautiful – and short – voyage off the cliff.

Pixley winced as he turned around. "Ah. It appears we've lost them."

Idris let out an audible gush of air and slowed the car.

"Sorry!" yelled Pixley again. "I was mistaken. They've caught up with us."

Idris shifted into gear again. The car rattled and the gearbox squeaked.

Winding back and forth across a series of switchbacks, they reached the top of the hill. Despite Fina's queasiness as she peered down over the precipice, the view – with Lisbon sprawled out below – was breath-taking. The Tagus river ran alongside the red-roofed city, which disappeared into the lush green below. Nestled on an opposite hill, a castle peeked out of the trees. She recalled from the guidebook that they must be near the fabled town of Sintra.

Flying down a road winding to the left, Idris gripped the wheel and turned hard to the right. Fina scrunched up her eyes, her heart skipping. As they slowed, she relaxed and saw they were on a dirt pathway, invisible from the road.

A small windstorm ensued inside the car as everyone exhaled together.

Idris rolled down the window, looked out, and then ducked his head back into the car. "I think we've fooled them."

Ruby leaned forward. "Who was it?"

Idris shrugged as he laid his arm straight out over the steering wheel. "That car followed me into Lisbon and then found us again as we left the dock. But I haven't any idea who it might be."

"While we're all sitting here," said Pixley, "without a lot of forward motion, would you tell us why we're here? In Lisbon, I mean. Soon to be Estoril."

Gayatri held up a finger to her lips. "Shhh!"

They all looked at each other. Then outside.

"What's that noise? A growl," said Gayatri.

Pixley and Ruby snickered. "I suspect it's dear Fina's stomach," said Ruby.

Fina looked down at her legs. "I'm afraid it is. And it's in all of your best interests that I eat soon."

Grinning, Idris squinted out at the field next to them. "Well, I'm glad your stomach has more sense than the rest of us. It's a perfect place for a picnic. I have a rug in the boot, along with bread, cheese, olives and wine. What do you say?"

No one answered. At the word 'picnic' they had all already slipped out of the car.

Fina pulled out an extra shawl from her suitcase and tightened it around her arms. It was December, though not too hot and not too cold.

Idris spread out a large rug in a field behind a small copse. They'd be invisible to anyone along the road, though it seemed unlikely their lurking follower would find this road.

Clinking tiny tumblers together, Idris said, "To the dynamic quadruplets!"

Fina said, "To Idris!"

Ruby said, "To Lisbon!"

Gayatri said, "To friendship!"

Pixley said, "To wine, bread, cheese, olives, and good company!"

Fina stuffed a piece of white cheese into the crusty folds of a baguette. She tore off a piece of the sandwich with the abandon of a small dog tearing at a piece of meat. She didn't care. It tasted so good. And the olives and wine made it perfect. A small cloud floated through the blue sky, waving down at them and their turn of good fortune.

Idris sat with one knee up and the other on the ground. He

saluted them again with his glass and took a sip. "I've corresponded with a friend of yours, Ruby. His name is Ian Clavering."

Ruby spilled her wine but only lost a few drops from the nearly empty glass. "How did you meet Ian?"

The right corner of Idris' mouth lifted in a slow smile. "We have mutual friends. We met in London recently as we all work in the same circles. As you know, Estoril is a haven for exiles of all types – royalty, spies, revolutionaries, stars, and the filthy rich. It makes it an ideal place for the likes of us as we can watch, listen, and learn."

Pixley popped an olive into his mouth. "Is there a particular group of people we're supposed to track?"

Idris produced a stack of brown envelopes from his bag. He handed one to each of them. "Please read these when we reach the hotel, and then destroy them. Or at least rewrite them in code."

With a smile, Ruby nodded at Fina. "It's fortunate Fina has a photographic memory."

Fina sensed Idris staring at her. She didn't need to look at him to confirm it. "I'd be delighted to memorise them all."

Idris closed his bag. "Good. But you ought to all remember your own dossiers. Each of you will watch different people." He plucked a blade of grass and rubbed it between his fingers. "We believe there is a ring of wealthy and influential people – like a smuggling ring – designed to bribe government officials and use the intelligence services against anti-colonial interests."

"Such as?" asked Gayatri.

"Well, for example, you're all familiar with the British company that controls the world diamond trade. They've had to shut down mines in southern Africa, but new diamonds have been discovered recently in Sierra Leone. The price of diamonds has skyrocketed. This company was granted exclusive rights over the trade for the next ninety years. Local resistance is building. Other diamond traders are trying to sneak in past this company, to mine the diamonds themselves. It's a powder-keg situation. That's just one example."

"So you're saying this ring is connected to the British diamond company?" asked Fina.

"Yes and no. It's complicated. You see, some of the people involved have controlling interests in the diamond firm but need ready cash to suppress resistance, or stamp out the other smugglers. It's a way to do it that's not directly connected to the company, but still in the company's interests."

Gayatri wiped her delicate hands on a napkin. *The hands of a surgeon*, thought Fina. "What do they smuggle, in addition to diamonds, presumably?"

"In this case, it would be diamonds. But more generally, they smuggle gems, paintings, spices, tea, and so forth. Items in high demand at a high price. If you own a tea plantation, for example, and the workers strike, then you, as the owner, stand to lose money. So you need funds to hire mercenaries, bribe law enforcement – whatever it takes to suppress those workers. Similarly, if you have local government officials or others organised against the empire's interests – whether they be British or Portuguese – then you can expect they will try to quash resistance."

Ruby shifted and smoothed her dress. "But how is this any different than what normally happens? The wealthy and powerful often successfully persuade government interests – intelligence services or otherwise – to act in their favour."

"You're correct," said Idris. "The difference here is this network of owners works to protect their collective interests. Salazar's Portugal is a perfect place because his own attitude towards Portuguese colonies is even more horrendous than most. The Colonial Act of 1930 has set back Portuguese colonies

– Cape Verde, Angola, Mozambique, Guinea-Bissau, and Goa in India – many years."

Pixley held up a finger. "I wrote a story about some strange happenings in Guinea-Bissau, where local cocoa farmers had their farms seized by some colonial landowner. They were threatening to strike one day, and the next they found themselves landless. The local government had stepped in. No one could trace a direct connection, but it was pretty clear some pressure must have been brought to bear on the local government."

"Mmmh," replied Idris. "So the purpose of our surveillance is to find out more about how the ring works, and who is at the helm."

"May we open these now?" asked Fina, toying with the flap on her envelope.

"I'd prefer you to wait until you reach your room. This interlude has been most pleasant, but we must arrive in Estoril soon. I have a great deal in store for your evening activities."

4

Like a satisfied fat cat, the Hotel Mansão overlooked the sandy custard-cream shore of the Atlantic. Its gleaming white exterior matched its gleaming marble interiors, adorned with columns and modern curved furniture. Sea breezes drifted in through the tall windows.

While Idris spoke to the manager, Ruby leaned over to Fina. "This isn't a hotel, it's a palace! Have you ever seen anything like it?"

Fina whispered back, "No, and I'm certain I'll fall over a lovely piece of furniture and cause a scene. Or spill strawberries on the white rug."

As they stood in the foyer near the concierge desk, Idris addressed their small circle as if he were a tour guide. "The staff will escort you to your rooms. Most of the guests dine around 8pm downstairs, so I suggest you do the same. After dinner, we will adjourn to the famous – or infamous – Estoril casino. Fortunately, our friends all enjoy a flutter at the roulette table, or a round of cards, so we will join them. We'll have a New Year's Eve celebration tomorrow night."

Fina leaned towards Idris. "Will you join us for dinner?"

"Alas, no. I must vanish for the evening, to attend to other matters. Besides, my presence will only hamper your surveillance efforts."

Pixley chuckled. "You can say that again."

Fina punched Pixley in the arm. "I'm sure we all understand. Perhaps we will see you at breakfast?"

"I hope to enjoy breakfast with you. If all goes according to plan."

PIXLEY, Gayatri, Ruby, and Fina pranced up the broad marble stairs as if they were preparing for an elaborate dance routine at the summit.

Pixley unlocked his door in between Gayatri's room on the left, and Fina and Ruby's separate rooms on the right. "This place is too marvellous, dar-ling," he drawled. "When will they arrest us for impersonating hotel guests?"

Fina flung open the door to her room, overcome by the anticipation of what lay inside. She was not disappointed. Idris had arranged a sea view for all of them. From the palatial balcony, a cool breeze ruffled the translucent white curtains. Her clothes already hung in the open wardrobe, and a dressing gown lay on the monstrously large bed. A beautifully carved wooden archway led into a small sitting room.

After a bit of careless unpacking, she threw herself onto the bed and grinned like a Cheshire Cat.

A tap came from the adjoining door. Fina bounced up and let in Ruby, who twirled into the room and fell into a nearby chair. "I cannot imagine what's come over me, but I'm positively giddy as a goat."

"Must be the sea air. And the wine at lunch."

"Whatever it is, I feel marvellous. And everything is already unpacked. Have you read your dossier yet?"

Without moving from her comfortable position on the bed, Fina tugged on her handbag and withdrew the brown envelope. She waved it like a fan. "Shall I? Have you read yours?"

"Not yet. Go on. What's yours?"

Fina turned the envelope upside down. A slip of paper floated downwards, along with a raft of brown and green escudos. "Gobs of money. We won't need to steal the bread rolls from the breakfast table!"

Ruby grinned and let out a sigh. "Idris is very thoughtful. Much more thoughtful than Ian."

Toying with the flap of the envelope, Fina avoided looking into Ruby's eyes. "What did happen to Ian? You mentioned he was on his way home to the Bahamas but I didn't hear anything else."

"That's all he told me. An aunt of his was ill, so he didn't know when he'd return to London." She twisted her opal earring.

"But that's the nature of Ian's work – it means he has to toddle off suddenly. I know you, Ruby Dove. You wouldn't have it any other way."

Ruby's furrowed brow disappeared. "You're right. Besides, I intend to enjoy myself – with or without Ian." She shut the balcony window and returned to her chair. "Let's hear it."

A cough echoed in the corridor.

Fina lifted herself onto her elbows. "Though these rooms are sumptuous, I suspect the walls are thin, and the floors are only partially covered by rugs, so noise travels. Why don't you read it with me?"

Ruby sat on the bed as Fina held out the memo. It had been written in a careful, precise hand, quite unlike Idris' spiky writing.

· · ·

FLORENCE ARMITAGE
    Born: 1907, England
    Residence: Royal Palace, Bucharest

COMPANION AND SECRETARY to Princess Thalia, Queen Consort of Romania, since 1934. After finishing at Cambridge, Armitage was unable to find a position. Princess Thalia journeys frequently to London, where she met Armitage. Circumstances of initial meeting unknown. Not to be underestimated. Razor-sharp intellect.

LENA FIERARU
    Born: 1901
    Residence: Bucharest, often at Royal Palace

MISTRESS of the King of Romania, Charles II. Daughter of a chemist. Learned English at the request of the King, who also journeys frequently to England. Status is an open secret in Romania. Besotted by perfumes and small dogs.

Hendrik Vogel
    Born: 1900
    Residence: Amsterdam

IMPORTER-EXPORTER FOR ZUSTER CHOCOLATE, based in the Netherlands. Vogel's wife, Elke, accompanies him everywhere. Devoted to his work. Gambling weakness. Has been spotted at casinos around Europe.

. . .

As SHUFFLING and scraping noises came from the hallway, Ruby and Fina stared at the door. Fina slid off the bed and scampered over in her bare feet. She bent and peered through the large keyhole. A pair of legs in trousers moved to and fro, and then another pair appeared. They seemed to be wrestling with one another.

There was a loud thud as a body crashed into the door. Exchanging a worried look with Ruby, Fina straightened up and flung open the door.

5

———

Two men stopped and goggled at Fina. Their arms and legs were locked together in a wrestlers' embrace.

One man, in a brown leather jacket, let go and stood up, sending the other tumbling to the floor.

Ruby popped her head over Fina's in the doorway. The man with the leather jacket lit up when he saw Ruby's face.

He smoothed his already slicked-back dark brown hair. "My apologies for the disturbance. We, were, ah, well, you know. Just good fun in the corridor."

Despite this puerile excuse, Fina nodded her head in agreement, as did Ruby. The man was an Adonis with a sun-kissed face, in sharp contrast to his pale white arms. Must be a film star.

As neither Ruby nor Fina responded to the inane excuse, the other man, clad in a moss-green suit, offered his hand to them. He gave them a full view of his combed-over hairstyle as he bowed. "I apologise for the disturbance, ladies. I lost a cufflink, but we unfortunately – rather comically – bumped into one another." He held up the emerald cufflink as if it were proof of their encounter and popped it back onto the cuff of his sleeve. He bowed again. "I am Paulo Mariz. Hotel Manager. And this is—"

"I'm Jeremy Salter. A pleasure to make your acquaintance." The man winked at Ruby and unbuttoned his jacket. "I'm a pilot on holiday. Born and bred in Cornwall."

"I'd say by your tanned face you haven't been cold as a jelis in a long time," said Fina.

Ruby shot her a sidelong glance.

Jeremy hesitated. "Aye," he replied, though his brow furrowed. He opened his mouth to say something but closed it again when, across the hallway, a door creaked.

Out slipped a woman with an opera diva's build, bearing, and gait. Encased in a fantastic white silk dressing-gown with jade-coloured cuffs, she wriggled her toes in slippers with matching white feathers. The feathers quivered in anticipation of their owner's next move. Her elaborate, swept-up, jet-black coiffure must demand hours of maintenance. "I heard a noise," she said. "Whatever is the matter?"

No one answered. Far from being bothered by the silence, the woman appeared to revel in it.

Despite her enormous size and presence, she had tiny, delicate hands. As she held one out for Paulo and then Jeremy to kiss, Fina noticed it was half-covered by a ring with an opal the size of a roulette chip. The woman floated towards Ruby and Fina.

Her rouged full lips parted, revealing a dazzling smile. "I'm Iveta Da Silva, travelling with my daughter, Makeda." She pointed back towards her room. "Please call me Iveta. I can tell we'll be great friends. Especially you." She nodded at Ruby's pinprick opal earrings. "You also prefer the opal, I see. Were you aware that when one wears opal, a stone of eroticism—" She interrupted herself as she leered at Ruby. Fina's face flushed hot with embarrassment on Ruby's behalf. "When one wears opal, it is said to bring about faithfulness and loyalty."

Ruby stood transfixed. Fina stepped in. "Ruby's friends are as loyal as the day is long."

"So true." Pixley joined the ever-growing throng of people.

"Who's loyal?" Gayatri asked, moving down the corridor.

"My goodness, dear – er, Ruby, is it? You *do* have loyal friends. They run to you whenever they hear your name!" Iveta held out a welcoming hand to Pixley and Gayatri. Introductions were duly carried out. Gayatri and Pixley appeared impressed by this woman's presence. She thrived on an audience, though her eyes fixed only on Ruby.

Iveta's melodious voice continued on about her favourite subject. "Ruby. What a beautiful and fitting name. Did you know it's the stone of passion, power, energy, and love?" She prattled on without a pause. "You may wonder why I talk only of precious gems. It is because I am a jewellery designer. I have a positive *passion* for gems."

Pixley suppressed a giggle.

Ruby pulled her earlobe, a sure sign of discomfort. "Yes, my mother reminds me of the stone's meaning all the time." She cleared her throat. "And your daughter's name is Makeda. Isn't she the Queen of Sheba?"

"Ah yes, my dear! You're smart *and* beautiful. Yes, I prefer Makeda, but in Brazil some people dislike the name, so she uses her middle name, Mariana, at home. We travel a great deal, so it's a pleasure to call her Makeda when we are elsewhere."

Pixley leaned forward. "Do you travel to Portugal often?"

"I travel to the continent at least once a year to – how shall I put it? Selling is such a vulgar word." Iveta was now physically cornering Ruby.

Paulo and Jeremy had vanished. Fina turned to Pixley and Gayatri. "Have you two read your—"

With a sudden movement, Pixley held a finger up to his lips and waved Fina and Gayatri into his room. Fina glanced back at Ruby, who gave her ever such a slight nod, a sure signal they could abandon her to Iveta.

Pixley's room looked much the same as Fina's, though all his possessions sat neatly on one table.

Gayatri smiled at the three pencils Pixley had arranged in perfect order. "We ought to plan to meet in your room – it's more orderly than mine."

"It's a professional habit as a journalist. It helps me think. And it's especially useful when I have to leave at a moment's notice." After closing the curtains against the darkening sky, he offered them a drink. Both politely declined.

"So. Tell me about your dossiers." Fina flung a lazy hand over the armrest of an overstuffed chair.

Pixley pulled a sheet of paper from the drawer. "I suppose we can tell Ruby about ours later. Let's read mine first."

Gayatri padded to the entrance. "Wait." She rolled up a rug and wedged it underneath the door. "It will muffle the sound."

"Splendid idea." Pixley sipped his brandy and cleared his throat. "Salvador Carvalho. Born 1898—"

Gayatri held up a hand. "Not *the* Salvador Carvalho. Here?"

Pixley and Fina looked at one another hopelessly and then at Gayatri.

"He gave a marvellous lecture at Quenby College last year. I'm surprised you didn't attend, Fina. He's a historian from Goa."

Pixley smiled. "And he's a rabble-rouser – a leader in Goa's emerging independence movement."

Fina eyed a box on Pixley's dressing table. It looked suspiciously like it might contain chocolates. Surely the dinner hour could not be far off. She tried to focus on the task at hand. "Why is Carvalho here, in Estoril?"

"It is the seat of the Portuguese empire," said Gayatri. "Where's the best place for a revolutionary to hide?"

Pixley raised his glass. "Amongst the rich and famous."

The door handle rattled.

6

———

Gayatri bounced up from her chair.

"It's Ruby," came the voice from the hallway.

Ruby entered, shut the door, and leaned against it. "Whew. The woman is like a sudden blizzard – sneaks up on you and stops you in your tracks."

"Have a drink, dear." Pixley handed Ruby a brandy snifter.

"Thanks." She sipped it and smacked her lips. "The only reason I endured her attempted seduction was because she's on my dossier."

Fina looked up. "But you said you hadn't read yours yet."

"I took a peek. Her name ran across the top."

"Find out anything useful?" Gayatri asked.

Ruby shook her head. "I don't believe so. She's a specialist in diamonds and emeralds. Emeralds are mined in Colombia, so it's easy enough to purchase them in Brazil. And miners recently discovered diamonds in Angola – a colony of Portugal. I was struck by the fact that she spoke more about trading gemstones than she did about designing jewellery. But she was remarkably coy about why she's actually here."

"So we ought to watch her and watch for any discussion of precious stones."

Pixley picked up his sheet of paper once more. "Doutor Fausto Tavares is on my list. A brainy cove from Cape Verde – seems a likeable chap. But if he mingles with the dogs, he'll be bitten by the fleas."

A loud ringing came from the corridor, despite Gayatri's rug precautions.

Pixley sighed and put down his glass as if he had a never-ending stream of house guests. "What now?"

Gayatri flung open the door. People flowed past in a steady stream towards the stairs.

"Must be a fire!" Gayatri snatched her handbag and waved the trio out of the room.

A few guests sauntered past, while others dashed down the hall. Fina recognised one strolling couple. The chocolatiers. She realised the man was her quarry, Hendrik Vogel. Behind him were Princess Thalia and her companion, Florence, also taking slow steps towards the exit. The Princess's eyes were unfocused and she stumbled a little as she walked.

After polite jostling in the entryway, they all emerged onto the seafront patio. Despite the excitement, the crashing waves appeared to soothe the crowd. They milled about in circles, the same way Ruby did when she was mulling over a problem.

Fina pulled her shawl around her shoulders. It was Portugal, yes, but it was scarcely tropical. At least the evening's stars sparkled. She sniffed to see if she could detect any smoke in the air, but there were only delicious aromas wafting from the kitchen.

Pixley leaned over. "Fire, my foot. I'll wager my firstborn this is all a ruse."

Ruby and Gayatri huddled close to them.

"I agree it's a false alarm. Something in my gut tells me so," said Fina.

Paulo Mariz lumbered towards the crowd, as if he had arisen after sitting in an awkward position for a long time. He wiped his balding head with a handkerchief and stuffed it into his jacket pocket. "*Senhoras e senhores.* Ladies and gentlemen. We have had reports of a fire on the first floor."

Fina looked at her friends. It was their floor.

Paulo clapped his hands together. "However. We have investigated and can find no evidence of a fire. I apologise most deeply. You may all return to your rooms."

The crowd burbled and churned as they made their way back into the warmth of the hotel.

"Oh, pardon me. I apologise." A man in a white suit and tie touched Fina's arm.

Fina wiggled her trampled toe. "No need to apologise. It's a difficult situation." She held out her hand. "Fina Aubrey-Havelock. Pleased to make your acquaintance."

The bespectacled man, who appeared to be in his late thirties, shook Fina's hand. He sported slicked-back hair and a fluffy moustache. Although Fina disapproved of such facial wear, it at least added necessary structure to his baby face.

"Likewise," said the man. "Salvador Carvalho. At your service."

Gayatri stepped forward eagerly. But as soon as she came face-to-face with Salvador, she was uncharacteristically speechless. Fina had never seen Gayatri lost for words before – this professor must really be something special. Eventually, Gayatri managed a hesitant, "How do you do? May I say, your lecture at Oxford last year was simply marvellous."

Salvador unhooked his round, owl-like spectacles and squinted at Gayatri as if she were an apparition. Satisfied, he replaced them on his nose and gave her a warm handshake. "I'm flattered."

Distracted from this mutual appreciation ceremony by the smells emanating from the dining room, Fina popped her head around the door frame. A few guests settled back down to their interrupted meals. Candles and large, comfortable chairs festooned with colourful cushions softened the room's cavernous high ceilings and marble columns.

A breath of air tickled her neck. "Feens, I'm certain you must be ravenous by now, but we must dress for dinner. Someone famous said hunger is the best seasoning, remember?" said Pixley.

"Whoever said that doesn't understand my stomach."

7

———

A soft ballad floated from the dining room's grand piano.

The waiter installed the trio in the middle of the large room, while most of the occupied tables dotted the perimeter. Ruby preferred to sit with her back to the wall but they had agreed to the table, given its ideal location for eavesdropping.

Ruby scanned her surroundings like a lighthouse. "Are you certain Gayatri isn't ill?"

Pixley, clad in a fashionable white dinner jacket and black tie, shook his head. "I knocked, but she said she'd join us in a few minutes."

Fina stared at the menu and flipped through her Portuguese phrasebook. She looked up, trying to appear concerned.

"Dear Feens, please do focus on the menu," chuckled Pixley. "It's best for all parties involved."

Ruby tapped a painted nail on the menu. "*Amêijoas à Bulhão Pato.*"

"It's clams, white wine, and broth," said Fina. "A light dish."

"Perfect – sounds delicious. That's what I'll have."

Fina pointed at the entrance. "Look! There's Gayatri. Selkies and kelpies."

Wisps of hair bounced gently as Gayatri, clad in a green frock, padded towards their table. Out of the ether, a waiter appeared and pulled out a chair from the table. Gayatri plopped down and held her fingers to her temples.

Pixley put a hand on her arm. "Whatever is the matter?"

"It's vanished."

"What's vanished?" Ruby's eyes widened. "Your dossier?"

Gayatri's lips opened, but no sound came forth. Soft rivulets of tears streaked her face.

"It's not your fault," said Fina. "Might have happened to any of us. Did you read it before the alarm?"

"Yes. Though I only read the names – I didn't have enough time to read the descriptions. The names were Elke Vogel and Princess Thalia. I can't understand it. I'm sure I locked my door."

Pixley clapped his hands. "Smashing. It's no great loss, Gayatri. Really. We've identified both of them. Besides, our dossiers don't have any major revelations. Knowing their names is enough."

As if in answer to Pixley's proclamation, Elke and Hendrik Vogel settled at the table nearest them. Elke wore a sumptuous red satin pyjama-like outfit and her husband a dark suit with a periwinkle tie. Fina suspected the tie was his wife's touch. Elke snapped at the waiter, "Mineral water, *por favor.*"

Covering one side of his face with a menu, Pixley whispered, "She knows what she wants."

Fina leaned over so far her hair nearly caught fire on a candle. "That's Elke and Hendrik Vogel – I noticed them in Lisbon at passport control. Hendrik is on my dossier."

Gayatri sniffed. "You mean I must attach myself to that rude woman?"

"She's certainly direct," Ruby said. "And knows what she wants. If she were a man, we'd think nothing of her behaviour. Besides, she has marvellous clothes."

"It's rather unfortunate they speak Dutch."

"I suspect Idris assigned me to Elke because I know a smidgen of Dutch."

The waiter arrived with steaming dishes of aromatic rice and soup. Fina forgot everything as she focused on her plate. She wasn't the only one – the table was silent save for a few slurps and smacks.

A shriek echoed around the room.

They all dropped their spoons with a great clatter.

In the doorway stood Iveta, wringing her hands as if she were about to sing an aria. Her rapid-fire Portuguese soon turned into English as Jeremy Salter joined her, Paulo at his elbow. "Whatever is the matter?" he asked.

The sleeves on Iveta's gown ballooned as she flapped her arms upwards. "What is the matter? I'll tell you. Someone has stolen my daughter's necklace!"

A slim young woman in a plum frock slipped in behind Iveta. Her oval face with broad eyes held no make-up save a light pink lipstick and a dramatic eyeliner. Not a hair escaped a high, tight bun. Fina guessed she couldn't be more than seventeen, though she would pass for mid-twenties if she had on more make-up.

Iveta turned around and grasped the young woman, squeezing the gold bracelet encircled around her upper arm. "My daughter's necklace. Makeda, tell Mr Mariz what happened."

Makeda clasped her hands in front of her and then behind, as if they were bothersome appendages with a mind of their own. She sidled closer to her mother. "I had the necklace in my hand when the alarm sounded. I set it down on the dressing table. When I returned, it had vanished." A bit of her mother's theatricality emerged when she pressed her fingers together and them opened them, mimicking a magician.

"I am deeply sorry to learn of this, miss." Paulo turned to Iveta. "Madam, but we did ask you to avail yourself of the safe." Paulo bent over so far in apology that Fina worried he might topple over.

"*Your safe*?" Iveta's voice reached its upper octave range. All of the diners went silent. Though Iveta was furious, Fina detected the tiniest of upward curves at the corners of her mouth. She enjoyed the attention. "How could we have used the safe when we had just arrived? Besides, my Makeda was going to wear the necklace, not leave it in the room. And pray tell, where is this fire?"

Even from this distance, Fina could make out pellets of sweat on Paulo's forehead. "I regret it was a false alarm, madam. But we must take precautions."

"I agree with you, Mr Mariz." Jeremy nodded. "But it's also true we have a thief in the hotel. If someone stole Miss Da Silva's necklace, it's possible other items have vanished as well."

What little colour remaining in Paulo's pallid face now drained completely away.

Gayatri leaned over the table and whispered, "Ought I to tell him about the thief in my room?"

Pixley and Fina nodded. But Ruby shook her head.

Pixley pulled his chair in closer. "Yes. It will put the thief on guard. And will make them aware we're watching."

"I disagree," said Ruby. "It's better to remain unobtrusive and incognito for as long as possible. Let them think we didn't notice – or better yet, that Gayatri wasn't aware the envelope was valuable."

Pixley sighed. "You have a point. Perhaps it's better we remain as innocuous-looking as possible."

A sumptuous and fleshy woman in high heels and a low-necked gown – one that revealed her décolletage most adequately – cruised into the room. She ogled Iveta, not in a licentious manner, but as if it were time to size up the competition. Her smirk indicated that while Iveta was clearly in her league, she still felt secure in her position as belle of the ball.

Pixley licked his lips. "If looks could kill…"

Fina pressed her fork into the bed of rice and octopus. "Why are women so catty and competitive?"

"Darling Feens. Your outrage is admirable, but I rather enjoy the sparks."

Gayatri smiled at Fina. "Ignore him. You know perfectly well why they're glaring at each other. It's because men cause us to compete with each other."

"Touché," chuckled Pixley, as Ruby gave him a gentle nudge in the arm.

A distinguished gentleman in a paisley cravat and cream suit entered and hooked arms with Iveta. Her cry of "Fausto, darling!" rang through the whole dining hall. The pair of them sat down at the table nearest Ruby's seat. Makeda trailed behind. The fleshy woman sat down near Fina.

Something brushed against Fina's leg.

"Was that you?" Fina looked at Gayatri.

Before Gayatri had a chance to reply, the tablecloth twitched. Then it began to move. Dishes slid towards Fina, first slowly and then with increased speed.

8

Crockery shattered at their feet as Fina and Gayatri jumped up from the table.

From beneath the ruins of the tablecloth, a tiny, shaggy dog appeared and yelped at Fina, as if she were responsible for the noise. The blighter had yanked off the cloth!

"Cici, darling. Are those people bothering you? Yes, come here my *pui*." The woman with the décolletage rubbed her nose against the furry beast's.

"See here," intoned Pixley. "Your dog pounced on our table and you say *we* were bothering *you*?"

In a rare display of outrage, Pixley's forefinger quivered.

The woman stood up, her flame-red lips pursed in disapproval. She pointed at Pixley. "Remove them from the room." She spun around, seeking a waiter. One materialised, though he stood well away from her. He bowed. "They are also guests at the hotel, Miss Fieraru. I can relocate your table if you wish."

Ah, this must be Lena Fieraru, thought Fina, brushing damp grains of rice from her frock. The mistress of Charles II. Though she was not conventionally pretty, someone might find her flair for the dramatic attractive.

"I will not relocate!" Lena made the announcement as if the military had arrived at her home. "Young man, do you know who I am?"

Cici barked in agreement.

Ruby glided towards the waiter and whispered in his ear. He nodded and whispered back. "These guests must excuse themselves to change."

Lena thumped her fist on the table. "Are you implying this is my fault?"

The beleaguered waiter held up his hands, as if he were protecting his eyes from the glare of the sun. "No, no, madam. I am simply telling you there is no need to relocate."

Mollified, Lena sat down, scratched Cici's chin, and scrutinised the menu as if it were a dubious receipt.

Pixley stood firm. Ruby thrust her arm through his and gracefully pulled him away. Once at the bottom of the stairs leading to their rooms, he turned to Ruby. "I have a bone to pick with Lena. Why didn't you let me make a scene?"

"You already made a perfect spectacle of yourself." Fina dabbed at the red blotch on her frock. "I'd better change and soak this stain."

Gayatri put a hand on Pixley's shoulder. "Why this urge for a scene?"

"I'm restless. I wanted to make something happen."

Ruby sighed. "A false fire alarm and theft is not enough?"

Pixley ran a finger around his collar. "It only adds to the tension. Can't you sense it in the atmosphere?"

"Hey! That's my line," said Fina. "All I can sense right now is a sticky, wet frock. Let's change. We need to arrive at the casino soon."

"You all can change – I'll wander around the hotel."

Though Ruby raised one eyebrow, she turned and walked up the stairs with Fina and Gayatri close behind.

"WHAT DO you think of this gown?"

Ruby smiled as she dabbed Fina's frock with her favourite stain-remover. The sight of it never failed to make Fina shudder, as she remembered how that innocuous little tin had brought about those horrible deaths during their fateful Christmas visit to Pauncefort Hall. But Ruby never let the memories ruffle her feathers. Her focus was entirely on Fina's wardrobe. "The burgundy with beading is beautiful. Sophisticated and sensuous." She handed Fina a blue shawl. "Here, take this wrap. It goes well with that burgundy."

Gayatri slipped in.

"How did you get in without a key?" Fina walked over and touched Gayatri's red raw-silk skirt. "Fabulous material."

Gayatri smiled. "Thank you, my dear. The door was open."

"But it wasn't. Given all that's happened since we arrived, I've been extra careful. I turned the deadbolt as soon as we got in – I'm sure I did." Grasping the knob, Fina flicked the lock open and closed a few times. "Why, this lock doesn't go in properly. It's no use at all!"

"Good gracious," said Gayatri. "I wonder if it's the same with my door. That would explain the theft of my dossier."

Fina tried the lock again. "It's cleverly done. The door seems secure, but it will give with one good, hard push. That's deuced peculiar, if both our rooms have the same problem."

Ruby tapped her teeth. "We'd better put our valuables – whatever they might be – in the safe. And tell Pixley. I'm planning on building a little fortress in front of my door tonight."

Fina shivered. The window to the balcony was open. The light patter of rain soothed her nerves, but it was too cold to leave the window open.

A flash of red and purple flew before her eyes.

Fina ran across the balcony threshold. "Did you see that?" The rain fell gently on her eyelashes and fringe. She squinted into the darkness.

Gayatri joined her. "What is it?"

"I'm not certain. A flash of purple and red."

Ruby squeezed onto the balcony. "Was it a bird?"

"No – too large."

"I don't see anything," said Gayatri.

"Neither do I," said Ruby. She brushed raindrops off her gown. "Let's go. Our gowns will be ruined if we stay out here."

Gayatri shivered. "Refreshing. But who was on the balcony?"

Fina fingered the latch on the windows. "I don't know, but I will tie these windows shut tonight with bedclothes if necessary."

Ruby grimaced and nodded. "Someone is watching us, girls. Apparently we're not the only spies in Estoril."

"Watching. Looking. Glass. Spectacles," Gayatri's eyes fixed on the windows. "Nor are we the only ones who aren't who we say we are."

Fina waved a hand in front of her. "What do you mean? You look as sober as a judge. Whatever is the matter?"

"I've only just remembered. That man we met before dinner – the one with the spectacles, who trod on your toe, Feens. I don't know who he is, or what he's doing here, but as sure as God made little potatoes, I'll tell you one thing. He's not Salvador Carvalho!"

9

_____

"Por favor." The young man with wiry arms and wiry hair sat back as Pixley leaned over the reception desk and whispered, "There's a lady outside who came to dine at the hotel. I'm afraid she's taken a turn – would you arrange a car for her?"

The young man grimaced, set down his pen, and telephoned for a motor-car.

"Thanks ever so much. Would you tend to her? She's just outside."

Eyes narrowed, the receptionist spun his pen around on the desk.

Pixley sniffed. "She doesn't like the looks of me, I suppose."

The receptionist nodded, sighed, and padded out of the front door.

Craning his neck, Pixley grabbed the guestbook and spun it around, running his finger down it, moving past their own names to...

"Sir. Sir. Do you speak English?"

Pixley turned his head slowly. The pale, washed-out woman with a little red lacquer hat stood with her hands on her hips. Her mouth opened in an exaggerated parody of someone speaking to a deliberately obstinate child. "Princess Thalia requires a car to the casino. Please make the arrangements."

Pixley ignored her and returned to his task. The woman uttered "hmph" behind him, but the clacking of high heels soon faded away.

He ran his finger further along the guestbook. Finally. Room 223. Doutor Fausto Tavares. He replaced the guestbook and slipped away up the stairs. To room 223.

No light glowed from under the door. Fina's tip-off about the questionable locks proved invaluable – a sharp nudge opened the tall door to the suite.

Pixley removed a small torch from his pocket and switched it on. At first, he shone it around the room like a wild, erratic spotlight. Then, catching his breath and inhaling the sea breeze, he moved methodically about the room. First, he trained the light on the desk. On one side sat a stack of books in Portuguese, next to a sheaf of papers that fluttered gently in the wind. A cursory look at the papers revealed a series of receipts from various jewellers. Next to the receipts lay papers in Portuguese and English. The English one read 'Mathematical Properties of Language'. Tavares had delivered the paper at Cambridge two months ago.

Pixley took out a small notebook, flipped through to a blank page and wrote the title of the paper.

He stopped. A few voices floated in from the hallway.

Then came heavy, plodding steps. Closer.

Pixley gulped. He wiped sweat from his brow but stood frozen and stiff in front of the desk.

A scrape in the lock followed the jangle of keys.

The billowing curtains beckoned Pixley onto the balcony. He rushed through the windows and into the salty air. Just in time, too, as the room flooded with light.

Although it was large, most of the balcony was visible from

the room. Pixley squeezed his frame into one corner and swore off chocolate and pastries for the rest of his life.

"*Meu amor!* You look more beautiful than ever." Must be Fausto.

"Darling, flattery will drive you absolutely anywhere you wish."

Before Pixley could identify the voice, he recognised the woman's scent. Tabu. It had to be Iveta.

She continued. "But what is it that you seek, *querido*? This hotel holds so many memories for us both – though I'm curious why you sent an urgent message for us to meet. Did I buy a cat thinking it was a rabbit?"

Fausto's response was muffled.

Papers shuffled. The sound of liquid was followed by the tinkling of a spoon against a glass.

"It's chilly, darling. Please close the windows."

Pixley sucked in his gut and prayed.

The windows shut with a bang so loud it nearly made him fall over the balcony.

Drat.

Now muffled by crashing waves from the shore, the voices faded away.

He was well and truly in a spot as tight as a fiddle.

RUBY GLANCED at her elegant wristwatch. "Where's Pixley?" She paced in a small circle near the hotel's entrance.

"I knocked but there was no answer." Gayatri moved towards the stairs. "Shall I try again?"

Fina shook her head. "He's not there. I also tried the door to our adjoining room."

"Shall we find Idris and ask him what to do?" Gayatri smiled at Fina.

"He gave us instructions not to contact him, and to take a motor-car to the casino." Ruby halted mid-circle and pulled her wrap tighter around her slinky mauve gown. A daring colour for Miss Ruby Dove.

"I'm cross with Mr Hayford." Fina blew a puff of air at her fringe. "He's supposed to meet us now. And he made a silly decision to snoop – or get into trouble on his own."

Gayatri said, "But perhaps *he's* the one in trouble."

Ruby stopped. "I agree with Fina. Pixley is a grown man and he made his decision. He'll catch us up at the casino." As if to make her final point, she stepped across the threshold into the crisp evening air.

PIXLEY PEERED OVER THE BALCONY. The bushes below might cushion a leap into oblivion, but not enough to make him seriously consider the option. He took in the sizeable gap between this balcony and the next. There was a ledge, but it was narrow.

He scrutinised every inch of the balcony. One railing bulged at the base. Something was wrapped around it – a snakelike object.

A rope!

Pixley gulped in joy and incredulity. But how could he reach the rope without being seen?

The answer was provided for him, however, as he saw a flash of red and purple across the way. Someone was moving around the other balcony – perhaps they were having a cigarette.

Pixley crouched down and inched across the balcony.

At last, he reached the rope. The purple-and-red figure had vanished. His heart slowed from a piston in a steam engine to the pulse of a beating drum. A tug on the rope confirmed it was snug against the balcony. The long tail of the rope dangled near the bushes, though it was difficult to judge how close it came to the ground.

He had to take the risk. As a journalist, he had once watched someone lower themselves via a rope against the side of a building. Even though the building had been on fire, the person had slid down with ease. Onlookers had applauded, but the poor sod turned out to be a thief who had selected the worst possible moment for his evening activities.

With a deep intake of breath, Pixley channelled his friend the thief. He straddled the railing, finally finding his footing on the ledge. The view of the ground only made him dizzy, so he focused on the rope. He tugged at it once more and lowered himself carefully down.

Bracing his feet against the wall, he slowly placed one hand under another, even as the rope swayed side to side beneath him. He lost his grip for a split second and the rope began to slide between his hands. Plunging downward, all he noticed was his burning hands. With a thud, he landed in the bushes.

A few stars winked at him as he lay on his back.

And then his eyes closed.

10

———

Arm-in-arm, Ruby, Fina and Gayatri skipped into Casino Estoril. They gasped in unison as they entered the main room. Casino Estoril catered to gamblers from around the globe. What they all had in common was money and status – or at least pretensions to it.

The cavernous room resembled the interior of a grand cathedral rather than a casino. Colourful classical murals graced the high ceilings, complete with little cherubs who danced and winked at the foibles of the humans below. Blue mosaic tiles, plants, sofas and chairs lined the walls. An elaborate chandelier hung from the ceiling and lines of low-hanging lamps looked like spiders preparing to weave their webs.

One corner held card tables, while the middle of the room hosted two magnificent roulette tables that resembled well-kept gardens.

Ruby coughed and waved her hand. "The smoke is thicker than the fog in Blighty!" She smiled. "But everyone's clothes are *the end*. I'm tempted to dash back to the hotel for my sketchbook. Look at who's approaching us."

Gayatri's eyebrows lifted. Fina leaned over and whispered,

"It's Princess Thalia of Greece and Denmark. She was on the ship, though we never caught a glimpse of her until we disembarked, remember?" Florence Armitage trailed behind her, in that same red lacquer hat.

"Her gown is too divine, isn't it?" Iveta popped up between Ruby and Fina. They all turned and greeted Iveta, resplendent in a tangerine off-the-shoulder silk evening dress, and her daughter in a figure-hugging emerald velvet gown. Makeda's eyes were alight with excitement as they darted around the room.

"We're here for a flutter at roulette, aren't we, darling?" In what was apparently her habitual sign of affection, Iveta squeezed Makeda's arms. "It's her first time at a casino. Too thrilling, isn't it?" She waved her arms about, as if she were revealing a secret society.

"Did the hotel find your necklace?" asked Gayatri.

"They are idiots." Iveta pointed at Paulo Mariz, who was having a tête-à-tête in the corner with a member of the staff.

Ruby nodded in Paulo's direction. "What is he doing here? I thought he was the hotel manager."

"Darling, Paulo Mariz is everywhere in Estoril. He manages the hotel and has a hand in running the casino. He also owns a fantastic perfumery in town – you must visit." She lowered her voice and stared at a cherub on the wall. "Yes. Yes. He has his, how do you say? His finger in every pie, that one."

"Am I late to the party again?" Jeremy Salter sauntered up, letting his cigarette hang from his lips as he talked. Fina's heart skipped. He was devastatingly handsome.

Iveta grabbed Jeremy's arm in a sideways embrace. "*Carinho*, Jeremy. You always arrive fashionably late, don't you? Remember that time in Monte?"

A bit of cigarette ash fell onto the floor. As Jeremy's eyes slewed around the room, Gayatri handed him a glass ashtray.

"Thanks. What was your name again?"

"Gayatri. Gayatri Badarur." She paused. "You've been to Monte? I adore it. Perhaps we've met before?" Gayatri fluttered her eyelids.

Fina tried, without success, to close her gaping mouth. Gayatri was an excellent actress.

Jeremy turned away from Iveta. Interesting that he hadn't responded to her.

"I'm afraid not," he said to Gayatri. "I would remember such a beautiful face."

Fina swore she heard a little snort coming from behind her. Ruby.

"Pity. I'm always looking for someone to fly me around. Have you been a pilot for a long time?"

"Ages. And you? You look too young to be an old hand at roulette."

"My family is royalty, so I have had a chance to visit Monte – as one does, of course."

What a brazen liar, thought Fina. Her stomach convulsed; a sure sign she was about to have a serious case of the giggles.

"Naturally." He puffed on his cigarette.

"Do you fly back and forth to Monte?"

He folded the remainder of his cigarette and smashed it against the ashtray. Something about this unusual ritual unsettled Fina.

"Yes, Paulo often hires me. Usually to shuttle guests." He coughed and spread out his hands. "Say, shall I take you up in my aeroplane tomorrow? The view of Lisbon and the shoreline is spectacular."

Ruby and Gayatri nodded eagerly. Fina's head remained still. She was not fond of aeroplane flights.

"Yes, yes, darling Jeremy. I'm sure these young things will enjoy that. But now, we must focus on winning! Winning at roulette!" sang Iveta as she glided towards the roulette table. Makeda and Jeremy trundled after her.

Gayatri followed suit, but Ruby touched her on the shoulder. "To the bar, girls. Time to quench our thirst."

Fina ran to catch up with Ruby. "Why the bar? Shouldn't we be watching everyone in the main room?"

"Yes, but they're not going anywhere in a hurry. Did you see that man who just went into the bar? He was at the table next to ours at dinner – Doutor Fausto Tavares. If memory serves, he was on Pixley's watch list. It's too loud to overhear conversations in the main room right now. We ought to keep an eye on Fausto, since Pixley isn't here yet."

"Speaking of Pixley, I'm beginning to worry." Fina turned around. "Where's Gayatri?" She peeked around the corner into the main room. Gayatri stood at the roulette table. Fina had never seen that expression on Gayatri's face. Her eyes widened and then squinted in intense concentration.

Ruby came up beside her. "Oh dear. I've seen that look before. My cousin had it when we used to wager wrapped sweets when we played cards." She turned towards the bar. "We've lost her for the time being. Let's hope she doesn't have too many escudos with her."

The bar was a welcome change from the controlled chaos of the main room. The low-ceilinged room was awash with thick, plush rugs. Hushed conversations were barely audible amidst the decadence.

A confident bartender rattled a silver cocktail shaker behind an array of gleaming highball glasses. Ten round tables with tall, plush chairs sat in two rows, so everyone could track who made their way to the bar.

Doutor Tavares reposed at table near the bar. A glass of *porto* sat untouched at his elbow as he scrutinised a sheaf of papers covered with hand-scrawled diagrams and mathematical equations.

Fina wriggled onto a bar stool. About halfway through the exercise, she gave up her studied insouciance and climbed onto the stool as if it were a horse. Ruby had no trouble sliding gracefully into place.

The bartender, who seemingly had four arms, nodded at Fina while he sliced a lemon, shook a drink, and poured a concoction into a highball glass. "Pink gin, please," she said.

He glanced at Ruby. "Martini. Three olives, please."

They turned and surveyed the scene. A piano struck up a soft jazz ballad. The high-backed, winged velvet chairs were so all-concealing that Fina could only tell which ones were occupied by the streams of smoke floating up from the tables.

Elke's blonde head shimmered in the candlelight near the door. Arms crossed, she marched to the nearest table.

Hendrik trailed behind her. "Don't lie to me!" he hissed. "I saw you with him. You've been lying to me all along."

Elke swung round and released her arms, lowering her shoulders at the same time. She put a hand on Hendrik's arm. "Dearest, please calm down. I can explain, but let's not discuss it here…"

They vanished behind the high-backed chairs.

Fina raised her eyebrows knowingly to Ruby, only to be met by an almost identical expression on her friend's face. A classic married couple's tiff. She wondered whether the 'him' in question might be another guest at the Mansão. Luxury hotels certainly seemed to bring out the worst in people.

Ruby sipped her martini and nodded towards the Doutor's table. Fina nodded back, giving her tacit permission to go and question him.

As Ruby slipped into a chair at his table, Fina turned her back and watched the master mixer ply his trade.

"May I buy you a drink, stranger?"

Startled, Fina spun round and would have tumbled to the floor if it weren't for Idris' strong grip. A tiny electric shock prickled up her arm. She whispered, "What are you doing here? Weren't you supposed to be in disguise?"

He grinned and blew warm air into her ear. "I had to see you. And I am supposed to watch you all tonight from afar. I tried on a bearded disguise but it was utterly ridiculous. Fortunately, none of these people know me. At least, that's my assumption."

"But should you be seen with us?"

"I had to chance it. When you and Ruby slipped into the bar, I decided it was a perfect opportunity to steal a few moments with you. They call this the spy bar for a reason."

"Spy bar?" Fina said the words a little too loudly. Elke's blonde head peered out from behind her chair.

Idris chuckled and nursed a glass of cognac. "Yes, yes. It's the spy bar because you can have a quiet conversation and not be overheard," he whispered. "Of course, it requires whispering."

"But surely that's not enough to call it a spy bar. There must be spies in it."

He winked at her. "And, who, pray tell, are we?"

Clickity clack. Fina bolted upright from her cosy position with Idris at the sound of high heels coming from the hallway.

He held a finger to his lips, smiled, and vanished from the bar.

It was Florence Armitage, in her red lacquer hat. She marched up as if she were about to demand a refund for a defective wristwatch. *Not to be underestimated,* Fina told herself, recalling the notes about Florence from her dossier. *Razor-sharp intellect.* Well, we'll see about that. Fina braced herself to carry out some adroit detective work on her quarry.

While Fina's brain spun round in circles, trying to concoct an opening gambit, the bartender came to her rescue.

"*Boa noite,* Miss Armitage. And how is the Princess this evening?" He inclined his head confidentially towards Fina. "Have you met Princess Thalia? We have all kinds of royalty come into the casino, but she is most special."

Florence pursed her lips. Fina couldn't tell if Florence found this flattering or merely invasive.

"Princess Thalia?" Fina sipped her pink gin. Delicious. "Was she not aboard the *SS Porto*? We arrived on the same ship."

Florence surveyed Fina for the first time. Her clear blue eyes narrowed. "That's where I saw you – you were on the ship." She twisted the stem on her glass of bubbly. Though her blonde eyebrows and lashes made her face appear adrift – save her rouged mouth – she had a kind face. Then she laughed like a burbling fountain. "I shut the door in your face today, didn't I? When we were aboard the ship?"

Fina saluted her with her glass. "Correct. It's my fault. I didn't realise the cabin belonged to the Princess."

"I apologise. It's my job to be overprotective. The Princess is often nervy. She has enemies."

Fina leaned in, making the most of this conspiratorial moment. "But she seems so delightful – from what little I've seen of her."

Florence put her elbow on the bar. Fina wrinkled her nose at the acrid odour of alcohol. This must not be her first glass. "She has political enemies, of course. As new queen consort to Charles II – though we still call her Princess – her enemies are Romania's enemies, Denmark's enemies, Greece's enemies, and other anti-royalist factions."

"But you're suggesting she has other enemies."

Florence sloshed champagne onto the bar as she waved her glass. The bartender immediately wiped up the mess. "We women have enemies, naturally."

"Naturally," said Fina, though she had no idea what she meant.

"That cat. That vulgar, immoral loose woman. Here, in the hotel!"

Elke's blonde head popped up again.

"Who?" asked Fina.

"Lena Fieraru. Daughter of a low-life chemist. It's bad enough for the King to have a mistress – though I suppose it's expected on the continent – but a lower-class woman of dubious moral character?"

"Are you saying everyone knows about his affair?"

Florence snorted. "He practically flaunts it. As does she. It's disgusting."

Fina changed course. "How long have you been the Princess's companion?"

"Three years. We met in London and I was looking for a companion or secretary position. She hired me on the spot."

"That was chancy, wasn't it? For her, I mean."

"What are you trying to say?"

"Oh – I, er, meant there must be an elaborate vetting process."

Mollified enough by this reassurance, Florence took another sip of bubbly. "I underwent an elaborate vetting process. I assure you."

The bartender gave Florence a slight nod. She blinked at him. Then she jumped, apparently realising he had requested payment. She rummaged in her handbag. A bottle of perfume spilled out, along with loose change and two bottles of pills.

While Florence paid the bartender, Fina scooped up the dislodged items. Eyes wide, Florence slurred, "Sorry. The Princess's pills. Helps calm her nerves."

A loud thud echoed across the marble floor.

Fina leapt down from her bar stool and rushed to the foyer, followed by nearly everyone in the bar. As she skidded to a halt, she almost bumped into Gayatri, who was rushing in with the crowd from the casino.

"Pixley!" Ruby, Gayatri, and Fina yelled in unison.

Bits of greenery and twigs marred Pixley's dapper jacket. He was out cold on the floor.

Paulo loosened Pixley's tie and looked up at an attendant. "What happened?"

The attendant let loose a stream of smooth Portuguese, punctuated with staccato notes.

"What's he saying?" asked Ruby. Doutor Tavares stepped forward. Fina had an urge to adjust his still-askew cravat.

"He says this young man arrived a few minutes ago, smiling and talking. Then he swayed, fainted, and tumbled to the floor."

Jeremy Salter pushed his way through to the front. "Aren't you a doctor? I'm afraid I've never asked you about it."

Fina wondered about Jeremy's brain capacity. One moment he seemed especially sharp. The next, as dull as a butter knife.

Doutor Tavares smiled at Jeremy, as if he were an obtuse student. "I'm a Doutor of Mathematics – with an interest in linguistics. Unfortunately, the closest I come to a medical doctor is by examining the human tongue."

Elke, Ruby, and Hendrik lifted Pixley and carried him to a sofa. Ruby sat next to him and stroked his bald head. "Pixley," she whispered. "Can you hear me, Pix?"

His eyelids shot open with a rapid blink. "Where am I? Oh, I..." He grimaced at the crowd. Waving a hand at them, he said, "Thank you for your concern. I will be fine shortly. No need to worry about me."

The crowd returned to their various drinking, gossiping, and gambling activities. Out of the corner of her eye, Fina noticed the man who had introduced himself as Salvador Carvalho, hovering around a potted palm and looking a little bit lost. She resolved to keep a close eye on him. They could hardly confront him about his identity in such a public place, but all her detective instincts were aroused by his masquerade. He had to be up to something. But what? The man was so diffident and professorial that she could hardly imagine him as any sort of criminal mastermind.

Gayatri sat at Pixley's feet. "What happened? Did you run into a tree?"

Pixley brushed a twig from his lapel. "In a manner of speaking, yes." His eyes darted around. He whispered, "I went in for a bit of snooping. I wanted to learn more about Doutor Tavares, so I nipped up to his room. It was open – because his lock has the same problem – and I snuck inside. He had a few papers about mathematics and linguistics. Not much else of interest. As I was having a jolly search, he returned, in the company of Iveta Da Silva."

"No!" hissed Fina. "Why was she in his room?"

"Half a mo, Feens. Let me catch my breath. They were clearly old chums, but Iveta said something about buying a cat thinking it was a rabbit ... which could mean anything, really."

"And?" Gayatri twisted her plait.

"And nothing. When the blasted Iveta woman closed the windows, I was stuck on the balcony."

Ruby giggled. Soon Fina and Gayatri joined in.

"Yes, yes, that's right. Laugh at me. Have a laugh at my expense, why don't you? Everybody likes to laugh at Pixley."

Though tears of laughter were streaming down her face, Ruby said with concern, "I'm sure we're very sorry, Pix. It's quite an image, you must admit. And the good thing is, you're safe and sound."

"Well, that's just it. It isn't the end of the story. Not by a long chalk. I was stuck on the balcony – wedged in the corner – when I spied a flash of purple and red on another balcony."

Gayatri gasped, and for a moment Fina felt afraid she was about to faint in her turn. She leant forward over Pixley, her plait swinging down to brush his chest. "Did you say purple and red?"

12

———

"Yes," said Pixley, "why?"

Fina clapped her hands. "I saw it too!"

"Well, that's doubly peculiar. A figure in purple and red was flapping around on another balcony – though I'm uncertain it was even a person. I crouched down so they wouldn't spot me," said Pixley.

Gayatri's brow furrowed. "But wouldn't they assume you were using your own balcony?"

Pixley groaned. "That didn't occur to me at the time – instinct kicked in and I had to escape. A rope was attached to the railing. I made it halfway down and then plunged into the bushes."

"Who tied a rope to the railing?" asked Fina.

Pixley shrugged. "I'm eternally grateful to whoever put it there." He sat up and rubbed his hands together. "What are we waiting for? We have work to do."

Ruby crossed her arms. "Some of us have been working hard, Mr Hayford. In fact, I had a delightful conversation with one of your lot – I mean your dossier lot – Doutor Fausto Tavares."

Pixley wiped his head with Gayatri's handkerchief and began his favourite imitation of an old soldier. "Thanks, Ruby. Awfully good of you, what?" He turned serious again. "Did you find out anything useful?"

"Not much more than you learned from your night-time excursions. Fausto's terribly interested in Cape Verdean culture and history, so I had to tread lightly as I have little knowledge about it. He certainly is a charmer, though."

A waiter approached and cleared his throat. "Forgive me for interrupting, but you are to collect your jetons from the head of house." He pointed at a small booth in the corner.

"Ah, must be a message from our host," said Gayatri as they moved, en masse, towards the booth.

"Jetons are roulette chips?" asked Fina.

Nodding, Gayatri stepped up to the booth. The tiny grizzled man who peered up at them from within looked as though he lived in the booth year-round. In the corner, Fina spied a small hotplate with instant coffee, alongside bread and cheese.

Without a word, the man expertly slid out metal trays of clay chips in a variety of colours – red, green, and gold. He pointed to each of them when it was their turn to retrieve their chips. Gayatri already had a tray full of chips, so she stacked her new treasure atop the old tray.

The tiny man pointed at the largest roulette table and shooed them away.

People swarmed around the table like bees around a honey-pot. Gamblers sat in rows either side of the table. Still more pressed in, constantly moving in and out, placing bets, expressing profound joy or regret, retreating momentarily, only to return in a few minutes full of hope that they would win a great fortune this time.

Drinks in hand, the Vogels came in from the bar. Hendrik had calmed down somewhat, but his jaw was still set rock-hard, and there was a nasty glint in his eye that Fina didn't like. He marched towards the booth for chips while Elke, muttering something, turned and left the casino.

Pixley whispered, "I haven't a clue about how to play. Do any of you?"

Ruby and Fina shook their heads. Gayatri grinned. "Absolutely. My father taught me. We went to a London casino last year. It was wonderful!"

"Teo!" called Hendrik to the croupier, with his usual air of one who expected to be obeyed. "Keep an eye on my chips, will you please? I must get some cigarettes." Leaving the tray of chips on a ledge by the croupier, he stalked back out to the foyer.

Gayatri gently pushed aside a few observers who were not placing any bets. She set her chip tray down at the edge of the table and waited for the trio to form a semi-circle around her. Then she pointed at the croupier: a ridiculously handsome young man who looked like a film star. "He'll call for the bets. The wheel has thirty-seven numbers, with only one zero. This is the European version, not the French or American version. The zero is marked in green on the wheel and the other numbers alternate red and black."

Pixley pushed in closer to the table. "What do the words impair, manque, pair, and passe have to do with the bets?"

"Don't worry about it right now. Watch for a moment."

Gamblers slid their chips onto the table. Fina was so caught up in the excitement she forgot to pay attention to the guests on her dossier.

Nearest the croupier sat Princess Thalia. Her impeccable posture contradicted the excitement flickering across her face. Florence Armitage stood next to her, ready to reach across the table to place the Princess's bets.

Next to Florence stood Doutor Tavares, who stared at the board while flipping over a chip in his hand. His cravat was still askew. 'Salvador' sat next to Tavares, empty-handed. He glanced around at the other gamblers, studying them as if they were animals in their own environment.

Jeremy Salter ran his fingers through his hair. The fingers quaked slightly, like a man who loves his drink but hasn't had a pint of beer in a fortnight. Iveta and Makeda stood a little to one side, almost indifferent to the proceedings. The three trays of chips stacked next to them proved otherwise. Lena Fieraru leaned back from the table, though Fina suspected she wanted to stay out of the Princess's sight. Lena gripped a stack of chips as if they were trying to escape. She was joined by Hendrik, cigarette case in hand, who pushed his way in beside her, squinting at the red-and-black numbers.

"*Faites vos jeux*. Place your bets, *kérem*." The croupier's voice had a world-weary edge. He sucked on a cigarette as if he were taking one last gulp of water before a marathon. The scar across the young man's temple made him seem like an older man who has seen too much of life.

The croupier spun the wheel.

Gayatri kissed one of her chips and laid it down between 2 and 5. Then placed more on 16, 21, and 34.

Fina whispered, "Why are you placing so many bets? I thought you only chose one number."

Without taking her eyes off her precious chips, Gayatri replied, "I think it's safer to spread the numbers around. Then you'll have a better chance of winning."

"But you win less, correct?"

Gayatri's eyes slid sideways, as if Fina had gone soft in the head.

Fina chuckled. "Sorry. I am a complete ninny when it comes to roulette."

Gayatri frowned as Pixley put a stack of chips on 13. Ruby put a hand on his upper arm. "Why select the most unlucky number on the board?"

"In point of fact, number 8 is most unlucky," said Gayatri. "Though putting all my chips on one number makes me nervous, I think 13 is a fine choice."

Pixley beamed. "Thirteen is lucky in Italy."

"We're in Portugal," whispered Fina.

"I'm aware of that, you bright young thing, but it's better to put it all on an unlucky number. You know, stare down fate and all that rot."

Other gamblers around the table gawked at Pixley. The croupier sucked on his cigarette in amusement.

The energy around the table intensified as bodies stiffened, jaws clenched, and waiters waited patiently to remove empty glasses.

"*Rien ne va plus.* No more bets." The croupier flung the little white ball into the spinner.

After its frenetic dance, the white ball finally settled onto the wheel.

13

The stone-faced croupier looked up and then broke into a smile.

"*Noir* 13."

"Yes, yes, yes!" Pixley jumped up and down. The other gamblers looked at him with a mixture of amusement and disgust.

"Well done, Pix!" Ruby, Gayatri, and Fina each gave him a hug. As Pixley raked in the chips, waiters exchanged empty glasses for fresh drinks. After much sighing and readjustment, the croupier said, "Bets, please."

Fina looked up from the table. The Princess's ringlets shook. She rose from her chair, still with her regal bearing, and leaned over the table. Then she clutched her stomach.

Florence grasped the Princess's hand. "Whatever is the matter?"

The Princess pushed her away, lips pursed. Even though her head was bent over and hidden by her curls, it had become chalky white.

Paulo, who had been overseeing the proceedings, now dashed to Florence and the Princess. He whispered to Florence and led them to a mural-covered door in the wall.

The collective silence now broke into excited chatter. "Must have been something she ate," said Doutor Tavares solemnly, as if he had discovered a new mathematical theorem. Nearer to Fina, Lena murmured to herself in Romanian.

Iveta squeezed Makeda's shoulders. Fina translated Iveta's next question as "Do you feel ill, darling?" Makeda said nothing but gave her a ghost of a smile. Hendrik, looking anxious, asked a question in Dutch. No one replied.

The croupier had followed Paulo, Florence, and the Princess. Now back in front of the roulette wheel, he adjusted his suit and slicked back his hair.

"Ladies and gentlemen." He cleared his throat. "We believe the Princess ate something disagreeable. She is resting in Mr Mariz's office. Mr Mariz says we should continue the game."

Lena tossed one of her chips onto 23. Doutor Tavares rubbed a chip on his sleeve three times and then slipped it onto 15. Jeremy grabbed two chips and slid them carefully onto 22. The man calling himself Salvador fluffed his moustache and looked gleefully around the table, but gave no sign he was ready to play. Iveta pointed at 5 and young Makeda dutifully slid three chips onto it. Hendrik bit down on a single chip – hard – before tossing it onto 21. His mouth curled up in disgust and he snatched up his drink, taking a large gulp.

This time, Fina hesitantly slid one chip onto 25. Her brother's lucky number. She'd play for Connor – she imagined how much fun he would have been having tonight. And he would have been the life of the party.

Ruby placed her bets on 1, 11, and 31. Methodical, cautious, and thoughtful.

Gayatri squeezed her eyes shut and laid her chip on the table. When she opened her eyes the chip was between two numbers so she put one chip on each number. "Time for a new tactic," she whispered to Fina.

Pixley let out the self-satisfied sigh of someone impatient with neophytes. He did not place a bet.

"Betting is now closed."

The croupier tossed the ball into the wheel, causing that delightfully delicate pinging noise, followed by suspenseful silence. Fina couldn't look at the wheel.

"Twenty-five."

Fina turned around and shrieked with joy.

Another shriek interrupted her celebration. Not of joy, but of terror.

14

———

"Help me alstublieft!"

Hendrik crumpled like a rag doll behind the roulette table, leaving only the sound of his choking behind.

Elke rushed in from the hallway, letting her handbag fall to the floor as she dropped down next to Hendrik's shaking body.

"Someone do something!" she shrieked. "Call a doctor!"

Half of the gamblers stood near the roulette wheel, while others had already made their way to the end of the table.

Jeremy, Iveta, Salvador, the croupier, Paulo, Gayatri, and Lena crowded around Elke and Hendrik. Elke stood up and then wavered. Iveta leaned over and caught Elke before she fell. Her arms encircled Elke like a straitjacket. It seemed to have the effect she intended. Elke stood still, though her hair fell over her eyes as her head lolled to one side. "Hendrik," she whispered. "Hendrik, Hendrik."

Ruby and Fina peered over the corner of the table. Pixley stood behind them. "What happened?"

Hendrik lay on the floor, face flushed, gasping for air. Then his body went limp, arms and legs akimbo in a most unnatural way. His spectacles had fallen halfway down his nose, giving him the ridiculous air of someone passing judgment. Around his head was a ring of dropped roulette chips, creating an equally ridiculous halo effect.

Paulo and the croupier knelt down and loosened Hendrik's collar and tie. The croupier slapped Hendrik's face gently, while Paulo slipped his hand down to Hendrik's wrist. He looked up at the crowd and shook his head.

"*Morto.*"

Fina nearly tripped over Pixley as she stepped back. Wiping his head with a handkerchief, Paulo dashed into the hallway, presumably to call the police. Despite the confusion, Fina noticed Salvador slipping something into Jeremy's pocket.

Makeda slinked after Paulo. The croupier jumped up and put a gentle hand on her arm. "*Por favor.*" He looked at the crowd. "Everyone must stay where they are, please. Until Mr Mariz gives us further instructions."

Lena wriggled forward and waved a hand. "And just who are you?"

The croupier treated them to a bow of his handsome head while placing a hand over his heart. "Teodoro Rapozo, Madam. At your service."

"I say, Teodoro, what gives you the right to keep us here?" Jeremy stepped forward next to Lena.

"Please, sir, I follow Mr Mariz's orders."

Gayatri stepped forward. "Mr Rapozo, I am a medical student – please let me help."

Teodoro nodded, sighed, and relaxed his shoulders. "Please, please, Miss—"

"Badarur. You may call me Gayatri." Gayatri knelt down and waved Ruby closer. Fina stood near them, but with her back to Hendrik. The sight of him made her queasy.

Lena pushed forwards, past Teodoro. In a flash, Pixley was by his side, blocking the outside world. The other gamblers had clearly given up any hope of leaving and had arranged themselves artfully on the furniture around the perimeter of the room.

Heads turned as the door in the wall to Paulo's office opened. Florence squinted at the crowd as if she sought a port in a storm. "Whatever is the matter?"

Teodoro's voice boomed. "It's best you and the Princess stay in the office. There's been an accident."

Taken aback, Florence slammed the door shut – much as she had in Fina's face that morning.

Gayatri beckoned to Ruby, and together they leant over Hendrik's body for a few moments, hiding it from view. After a few sniffs, they nodded at one another and said in unison, "Cyanide."

Elke's face drained of what little colour remained in it. Her head slumped back onto Iveta's shoulder.

With his hands behind his back, Doutor Tavares bent over the corpse. "Correct. Bitter almonds."

Gayatri grimaced. Fina guessed she was reacting not to the odour but to the officious air of the doctor.

Moving aside a pair of owl-like spectacles, Ruby reached across the betting table for Hendrik's rack of chips and held it close, though she was careful not to touch the chips themselves.

The squeal of sirens broke the quiet hum.

Fina's heart thumped and her knees weakened. Where was Idris? Surely he must have seen the commotion. On second thought, he was wise to stay away.

The door flew open and a dapper man in a navy suit, broad moustache, and brown fedora rushed in, breaking Pixley and Teodoro's blockade. Nodding at the crowd, he said in a deep rich voice, "Comissário Cardoso, *Polícia de Investigação Criminal*. Please, ladies and gentleman, stay where you are. I will speak with you shortly."

A herd of uniformed police streamed in after him.

Once she had handed the rack of chips to an officer, Ruby put a hand on Fina's shoulder. "From my reading about the Portuguese police, he's quite high up. Although I suppose it's warranted."

"Our goose is well and truly cooked," said Fina as she looked at Pixley's forehead, dripping with pellets of sweat.

"Not necessarily."

Gayatri left her post as a horde of police surrounded Hendrik's body. Out of the corner of her mouth she said, "What do you mean?"

"Everyone else here has many more skeletons in their cupboard than we do. We'll all look like the innocent students we are. Except Pix, of course, who will get a bit of questioning as a journalist. But he can handle himself."

Gayatri tugged at her plait. "I certainly hope you're right, but I fear the worst."

Fina smirked. "Thank goodness there's someone who worries as much as I do."

A constable – or the equivalent rank – jumped up, causing the chairs nearest the body to fall on one another like dominos. Comissário Cardoso glared at the young man.

As if in response to the rebuke, the constable held up a slip of paper in triumph.

15

Comissário Cardoso snatched the paper away from the constable. Rubbing his forehead, he glided to a seat next to Elke. He took off his fedora, perched it on his knee and offered her the note.

"Please, Mrs, ah—"

"Vogel," supplied Iveta, wiping Elke's hair away from her face. Makeda sat next to her mother, arms crossed. She glared at Elke.

"Mrs Vogel, yes. Would you be so kind as to read this note in Dutch? We found it in your husband's pocket."

Elke sat up and held the quivering paper close to her face. Squinting, she put down the paper and rummaged in her bag. She pulled out a pair of pince-nez and perched them on her nose.

She ran her tongue along her lips several times. "He says: Dearest Elke, I must leave you. I am so sorry. Love, Hendrik."

Cardoso tapped his hat on his knee. "Well. Was your husband distraught, Mrs Vogel?"

Lips pursed, Elke shook her head.

"Can you imagine any reason he'd take his own life? Had he debts, money troubles or other worries?"

A stream of invective in Portuguese tumbled forth from Iveta. She glared at the Comissário.

Refusing to take the bait, Cardoso rose from his chair. He cleared his throat. "Ladies and gentlemen, you must be most distressed by this unfortunate occurrence. It seems Mr Vogel – how do you say? Took his own life."

Gasps. But Fina also detected sighs of relief amidst the noise.

Everyone gathered up their belongings.

Comissário Cardoso held up a hand as if he were directing traffic. "Please, I ask you all to remain where you are. We will need to ask you all a few questions and take down your addresses."

Paulo stepped forward, his head gleaming in the bright lights. "Comissário, all of the guests around the roulette table – except the croupier, Teodoro Rapozo – are guests at Hotel Mansão."

"How convenient," said Cardoso sardonically. He spun round like a top. "Who first determined that the means of death was cyanide? I would like to speak with you in the bar, please." With that, he glided out of the room, clearly expecting the chosen ones to follow.

Gayatri beckoned Ruby, Pixley, and Fina to come with her as she followed the Comissário. Fina drank in the cool night air that streamed in through the front doors. The main room of the casino was not only stuffy and hot, but as foul-smelling as a fox's cave.

An odd rush of reassurance flowed over Fina with the pleasing *tap, tap* of their shoes on the parquet floor. The bartender still stood in place, now arranging glasses on a tray. He whistled a little tune.

The Comissário took no notice of the jolly bartender. He

tilted his hat at a jaunty angle on the back of the chair, unbuttoned his blazer, and flounced into the seat.

He withdrew a cigarette, tapped it on the cover, whipped out a silver lighter, and had the smouldering stick between his lips in three seconds flat.

Pixley, Fina, Ruby, and Gayatri lowered themselves into the seats as if they were entering a hot bath.

Cardoso removed his cigarette and waved it at them. "Yes? Why are there four of you? I understood that two of you identified the cyanide."

Pixley adjusted a trouser leg and leaned forward. "We're all travelling together, so we thought it best we—"

"Yes, yes." Cardoso tapped his fingers on his knee. "Which one of you is the medical student?"

Gayatri raised her hand as if embarrassed to know the answer. "I'm Gayatri Badarur, medical student at Oxford."

She nodded at Ruby, who said, "I'm Ruby Dove, also a student at Oxford. In chemistry."

He turned to Fina. "I'm Fina Aubrey-Havelock. Just an Oxford student reading history."

Pixley chuckled, "And I'm Pixley Hayford, just a scandal-mongering journalist."

Cardoso turned back to the three women. Pixley sniffed.

"Tell me what happened, Miss Badarur." Then he held up a hand as if to stop himself. "First, tell me how three students – and a journalist – can afford to travel in this luxury?"

"I'm a princess," said Gayatri in a matter-of-fact tone. "My family had plenty of money to send me to Oxford." Little did Cardoso know that although Gayatri's family was royalty from Tezpur in Assam, they spent all their money sending her to Oxford.

Fina said, "My uncle wanted to send me away for the winter,

but I didn't want to go alone. I'm here for a seaside cure. He paid for us to spend New Year's in Estoril."

Cardoso's eyes bored into Pixley. "Let me guess. You're working on a story." Fina couldn't tell when this detective was joking and when he was serious.

"Quite right, quite right." Pixley cleared his throat.

Gayatri came to the rescue. "I'm afraid I was too focused on the roulette wheel to have paid attention to what happened."

"Did any of you see anything else? Anything at all?"

They looked at one another. Fina was just about to tell him about the exchange between the imposter posing as Salvador Carvalho and Jeremy Salter.

The Comissário harrumphed. "They say Oxford University students are so very clever, do they not? And yet you four noticed nothing! Not so clever after all, hey?"

She decided to tell him later, if at all.

Ruby smoothed her hair, "I noticed most of the gamblers had little ritualistic gestures as they put down their chips. Mr Vogel's was highly unusual." She paused. "He bit on his chip – inserting at least half of the disc into his mouth."

Cardoso's eyebrows lifted. "Go on, Miss Dove."

"Well, that's how he might have ingested the cyanide."

"But didn't he top himself?" asked Pixley. "Sorry. I meant committed suicide."

Cardoso held up another arresting hand at Pixley. "So he could have ingested the cyanide that way."

Gayatri frowned. "Mr Vogel had a whole rack of chips, and he left them lying about while he popped out for cigarettes. Anyone could have tampered with them."

The right corner of Cardoso's lip lifted. "Anyone who was there, that is. And only someone familiar with Hendrik's gambling habits could kill him."

"But Comissário, I—"

"Please, Mr Hayford."

Fina suppressed a snort. She envisioned steam issuing from Pixley's ears.

Cardoso continued. "But why poison the chips? Why not simply put cyanide in his glass?"

Ruby tapped her teeth. "Why, indeed. It must have been the easiest option. He had his glass with him the whole time, and I suppose it's risky to slip poison into a glass sitting in plain sight of everyone, even with the controlled chaos of the roulette table. So many things might go wrong, and it would be deuced difficult to be certain no one noticed you."

"Whereas with the chips, you could do it any time," said Fina.

"If this is true, the murderer has to be someone familiar with Mr Vogel. That ought to narrow it down enough, I would think."

A voice came from behind Fina's high-backed chair.

"I'm afraid not, Comissário."

The elegant detective turned his head. It was Teodoro Rapozo.

"You?" said the Comissário. "What have you to do with this affair? Did I ask you to accompany these people? No. If we have need of you, we will summon you, but now, *senhor*, you must return to your roulette table."

"Not mine." The toothpick between Teodoro's lips twisted. "You've made a mistake, Comissário."

"What's he on about?" hissed Pixley to Fina. She could only shrug.

"Not my roulette table. You see," Teodoro continued, "I'm not really a croupier."

16

____

Teodoro Rapozo looked at Ruby, Fina, Gayatri, and Pixley as if seeing them for the first time.

"Enough games!" said the Comissário impatiently. "Who are you?"

He sighed. "I suppose everyone will find out soon enough, so I might as well tell these four, too. I am Portuguese, yes, and I am in a way a croupier. The casino pays my wages. But I have another employer, a secret one: King Charles II of Romania."

The cigarette dropped out of Cardoso's mouth, missing his leg and falling onto the floor. Pixley picked it up and handed it back to Cardoso. Fina detected a thaw between the two.

"I see. Why did the King hire you?"

Teodoro flipped the toothpick to the other side of his mouth. "He was worried about the safety of his wife. And another friend of his – Lena Fieraru."

Ruby opened her mouth and then shut it. Teodoro smiled. "Yes, she is his mistress. It's an open secret in Romania, so there's no reason to keep it from you."

"But why become a croupier? Why watch over her at the casino rather than as staff at the hotel?" asked Ruby.

"I also work at the hotel during the day, though in a more discreet role."

"Are there particular threats against the Princess? Or Miss Fieraru?" asked Cardoso.

He nodded and withdrew an envelope from his pocket. "She found this in her room when she arrived at the hotel this afternoon. Princess Thalia's companion, a Miss Florence Armitage, gave it to me. The Princess is not aware I'm watching over her, but Miss Armitage knows. Of course, the Princess will find out soon enough."

Cardoso stuffed the envelope in his jacket.

Pixley crossed his legs. "Comissário. Sir. May we know the contents of the letter?"

"I don't understand why. You all are suspects."

"But you said it was suicide," said Ruby.

"That will be the story. And you all must keep quiet and go along with it."

Fina cleared her throat. "Though we may appear young and naive to you, sir – and undoubtedly we are young – we are experienced in these matters. We have solved a few crimes."

His eyes narrowed. "I do not approve of amateurs. We are a professional force here in Lisbon." He wagged his fedora at them as he stood up to take his leave. "Do not get involved. Do you understand?"

They nodded obediently.

"Tell no one it's anything other than suicide. And do not leave Estoril. Or I shall be forced to take serious measures."

~

"Teodoro. Mr Rapozo." Ruby crooked her finger at him and bestowed upon him her most dazzling smile. "Join us for a moment, won't you? I'm sure the Comissário will speak to you in good time."

He scanned the room, nodded and sat down. "What do you want to know? I cannot tell you much, you understand."

"Why did you imply everyone around the roulette table was already familiar with Hendrik Vogel?" asked Pixley.

Teodoro smirked and sucked in air through a gap in his front teeth. "You noticed that, didn't you? I was surprised the Comissário didn't ask more about that, but perhaps he'll ask me later." He moved forward in his chair. "The King's people gave me files on everyone at the table. Including the four of you." He winked.

The four friends exchanged glances.

"Don't worry," he said. "Your secret is safe enough with me. There's no reason to tell the Comissário because you four are the only ones who hadn't met Vogel before this encounter at the casino."

"Tell us all about the others," said Gayatri.

"That would be going too far." His eyes twinkled. "But I can tell you what was in the note the Princess found in her room, because it's in Her Highness' best interest she be protected. It said she had better watch her step."

Pixley pulled out his notebook and tiny pencil. "Those were the precise words? About her step? Was it in English?"

Teodoro's eyes flashed. "I'd prefer you not write this down, please." Pixley closed the cover on his notebook. Teodoro nodded. "Yes, it was about her *step* – in English."

A constable marched into the bar. "Please come. Everyone is to leave the casino. Questioning, if necessary, will begin again in the morning."

FINA RUBBED sleep from her eyes and blinked in the darkness, disoriented by the complete absence of light and a mild night-mare in which she had been covered in treacle – or was it honey? – and unable to move about. She sighed, brushed her fingertips against her arm to be certain there wasn't any treacle or honey, and leaned over to switch on the light.

She struggled with the base of the lamp – where was the blasted switch? Her fingers brushed against something smooth and cold. Porridge-brain though she might be, she remembered the bedside table was empty, save the lamp and clock.

Heart racing, she leapt out of bed and fumbled for the light switch for the room. *Click.* The bedside table was indeed crowded with objects now. A green melon sat on the table.

A large gleaming knife protruded from the skin of the melon.

In a flash, Fina leapt out of bed. Afraid the knife might leap from the green flesh and into her chest, she pounded on Ruby's door. Then Pixley's. "Help! Ruby... Pixley!"

Pixley was the first to enter, like a bear awoken from a pleasant stretch of hibernation. Somehow, he had found his way into the room without the aid of his eyesight. He lumbered over to Fina's bed and hovered, swaying from side to side. "What is it, young trout? It's too early for dashed emergencies."

Ruby entered next, in considerably finer form than Pixley. Her eyes were wide and her step was certain. She tied the belt on her dressing-gown so snugly it threatened to cut off her circu-lation. "What is it? I heard nothing – I woke up early and was reading in bed."

Fina pointed a quivering forefinger at the display on the table.

Pixley's eyelids flew open like a window shade. "Good Lord. Is that what I think it is?" He moved forward with exaggerated steps, as if he were afraid he would disturb his prey.

"It's too awful. I woke up and ran my hand across it in the darkness." Fina covered her eyes.

Ruby padded over and squeezed Fina. "If they wanted to hurt you, they could have done so quite easily, it seems."

They both shuddered.

Pixley strode over to the window and opened the thick curtains, revealing a pale sky. Dawn was not far off. He fumbled in his dressing-gown pockets, finally locating his spectacles. "Hullo. What's this?" He slid a slip of paper from underneath the melon.

"'Stay away. Clear off.'" Pixley lowered his spectacles, tapping the tip of one ear-hook on the paper. "I suppose we ought to give them credit for being direct."

A tap came at the door. "Must be Gayatri."

It was not Gayatri.

17

Paulo bowed to Ruby, Fina, and Pixley, who shuffled to one side so that his body hid the melon from the manager's sight. "Please accept my most sincere apologies, but the Comissário requests your presence in the dining room. He has said not to worry – he has a few questions to ask over breakfast..."

"Of course." Ruby looked at Fina and Pixley. "We'll join him in a few minutes. Have you already awoken Miss Badarur?"

"No, no. He said he only want to speak to the three of you, so I haven't disturbed her."

"Yes, better to let her sleep, then." Ruby's brow furrowed.

Ruby leaned against the door as she shut it. "I wonder why he doesn't want to speak to Gayatri." She shrugged. "We'll wake her after we finish with the Comissário."

In fifteen minutes, the trio had dressed and performed as many hygiene tasks as possible. As they lurched downstairs, Fina asked, "Shall I tell him about the melon?"

Pixley nodded. But Ruby shook her head.

"Let's hear him out. No need to give him a reason to spend more time looking into our background."

Pixley sighed. "Ruby is correct. She's always correct, which is simply maddening."

Ruby chuckled. "Not in romance. I am sadly mistaken in reading any of those signs."

Pixley and Fina kept quiet. Fortunately, they soon arrived at the dining room.

The first oblique rays of sunlight were streaming in through the windows, enhancing the clean and fresh feeling of breakfast. The smell of bread wafted in from the nearby kitchen and mixed with the heady whisper-breath of coffee cups steaming around the room. Gentle waves, interspersed with jolly bird chirps, completed the idyllic scene. Only a few guests sat at the breakfast tables. It was too early for most of the casino nightlife-loving crowd to rub the sand out of their eyes.

Comissário Cardoso's table overlooked the gardens that rolled down to the sea. He sipped his espresso in between long drags on a cigarette. Unlike the rest of the trio, who'd had their sleep, the Comissário looked bright and singularly without tell-tale circles under his eyes. The only sign he'd been awake all night was the stubble spread across his cheeks and chin.

He stood up and clasped their hands as if they were old friends.

"Sit down, sit down. I've already ordered many breakfast dishes. If they are unsatisfactory, please order more."

A waiter approached with three cups of espresso, or *bica*. Fina smiled. She was ready to drink at least four cups, but the shock of the melon warning had already jangled her nerves.

"Are you here to share more news about what happened last night?" asked Ruby, her slightly high-pitched voice indicating this was a wish more than a question.

Cardoso scratched his chin. "Not precisely. But I will share with you that we found traces of cyanide in Mr Vogel's glass, as well as on his roulette chips."

"But he gulped down his drink right after he bit his roulette chip for luck," said Fina.

"And perhaps he did so because the chips tasted bitter," added Pixley.

"How does that alter the fact that the poison was in both places?" asked Cardoso.

Ruby wiped her hands on a napkin. "I think what they're saying is that Mr Vogel could have ingested the poison via the chips and then left residue in his drinks glass afterward."

Cardoso gave out a low, wheezy laugh. He wagged a finger. "It's true – you three are sharp. You've passed the test."

"What test?" asked Ruby.

"I heard the three of you have been involved in past murder cases." Cardoso delivered this news as if he were discussing the lovely weather. "I wanted to see if you could provide a more complex answer as to what occurred last night."

Pixley's cup clattered onto its saucer.

The waiter arrived with butter, ham, cheese, jam, and bread. Fina peeled back the napkin which encased the bread, causing a cloud of steam to rise to her nostrils. Consumed by the simple but glorious meal, Fina snatched a piece of bread and slathered it in jam as if she were racing against Pixley and Ruby. Ruby did not glance at her but gave a wry smile instead.

Cardoso puffed on his cigarette and let out a long stream of smoke. "So, you understand my hesitation to trust you very quickly."

Ruby set down her knife. "Who told you we'd been involved in murder cases??"

"A friend."

"You'll have to do better than that."

Though she was now intent on her cheese, Fina looked up at Ruby, impressed by her audacity. Pixley stared at Ruby, mouth hanging open.

Cardoso tapped his cigarette on an ashtray until it was pristine. "I checked up on the four of you. Miss Badarur is precisely who she says she is. But you three – well, you're not lying exactly, but you're not providing the whole truth, either."

"Mind your step." Florence's voice broke the thick layer of tension in the room. She held the Princess's hand as she piloted her through the maze of tables. Pale-faced, the Princess tottered towards her table, as if she were a desert-wanderer who had spotted an oasis.

As soon as they were safely ensconced in their chairs, Florence tipped out a few pills from a brown bottle in her bag. She handed them to the Princess, who washed them down with a swig of juice.

Fina turned her attention back to their own dramatic scene. Ruby laced her hands together, rested her chin on them, and gazed at the detective. "When Fina told you we had experience in these matters last night, you dismissed us as amateurs. So we didn't lie. You just didn't want to listen to us."

The Comissário shifted his legs, twisted his cigarette, then pulled his chair closer to the table. He beckoned them closer. "A visiting police officer told me you three had been mixed up in a number of homicides. And that you had helped to solve them."

Pixley glanced at Ruby and mirrored her gesture with his hands. "A visiting police officer? Seems highly unlikely, sir. You must try harder if you want to convince us."

The detective leaned back and threw down his napkin. "Fine. An intelligence officer from another country. When he learned about the death last night, he told me about you."

Fina's mind raced. Might it be Ian Clavering? Ruby's erstwhile boyfriend? Though he was in intelligence, he didn't work for a government – as far as they knew. She shook her head. This wasn't Ian's style. It had to be someone else. Someone they hadn't met before.

"So now that you know, you want us to help you," said Pixley.

"On the contrary, Mr Hayford. I must tell you that if I do find out you've been snooping and interfering with my investigation, I will be forced to take serious action against you."

"You mean you came to warn us? Again?" Fina asked.

Cardoso rose, buttoned his jacket, and slid his fedora onto his head. "After what my colleague told me, I decided to warn you again, since you apparently have difficulty following police instructions."

18

"Paulo said he would take us to his perfumery this morning." Gayatri stood behind a dining-room chair and propped her locked arms on the back. She wore a moss-green frock, with matching hat. "They're already in the foyer – Florence, the Princess, Iveta, and Makeda. Lena declined when she saw the Princess, and Elke is not in the mood."

"Are you rested? Would you like breakfast?" asked Fina.

Gayatri rubbed her stomach. "I slept in and then had breakfast in bed. What have I missed so far this morning?"

The trio looked at one another and burst out laughing. "Let's just say we've already had a visit from the police," said Fina.

Gayatri's eyes widened. "This will obviously require explanation, so why don't you—" she nodded at Ruby and Fina "—go along on the perfumery expedition? It doesn't interest me."

Pixley pouted. "What will we do in the meantime? Twiddle our thumbs? It's too cold to lie on the beach."

"I'm thinking strategically, like dear Ruby. At least that's what I'm trying to do. Though I must admit I'm itching to gamble."

Fina gave Ruby and Pixley a furtive glance.

Gayatri lifted the chair onto its hind legs. "No, I heard the man who isn't Salvador and the Doutor say they were going to the university in Lisbon this morning. To meet a few colleagues. I thought Pixley and I could follow them."

Pixley wiped his spectacles. "Won't they notice us?"

Ruby chuckled. "Those two are the epitome of absent-minded professors. Especially 'Salvador'. It's hard to believe he's up to nefarious purposes, given his hapless ways. They'll be so absorbed in conversation I doubt they'll notice us."

"Aren't we all forgetting something?" Fina set down her third *bica*. "Aren't we supposed to stay in the hotel?"

Gayatri shook her head. "Paulo told me the police are certain it was suicide – at least that's the official story. We're all to stay in residence at the hotel, but we're free to come and go as we please. They want us available for questioning."

"An excellent opportunity for the police to follow us." Ruby wiped her mouth with a cloth napkin.

Gayatri held up a finger. "I forgot to mention one other thing. Remember Jeremy and his aeroplane? He would like to take us up this afternoon. He can fit four passengers."

Fina's stomach turned. "Really? Perhaps it's better if the three of you go. I'll inspect the pastry shops near the hotel for miscreants."

"Nonsense." Ruby threw down her napkin. "You'll be fine, Feens – it's just nerves."

Florence's head poked around the doorframe. Today she wore a dove-grey hat, with exquisitely crafted silk flowers. Fina felt a pang of jealousy. Florence's collection of top-notch millinery must have cost a small fortune.

"Are you ladies coming to the perfumery?" Florence asked. "We're about to leave!"

～

THE CHATTY PARTY of women took two cars into Estoril. Iveta had convinced Elke it would be better to be busy than to sit alone. The Princess, Florence, Elke, and Paulo went in one car, while Ruby, Fina, Iveta, and Makeda went in the other.

Soon, they arrived at the now-famous Estoril arcade of shops. The guidebook description was apt: the shops were arranged in two orange half-wings, resembling a butterfly.

"The arcades have become famous since they were built a few years ago," boomed Iveta's contralto voice. "Ruby must be familiar with these shops – the clothes are simply to die for."

Iveta's flying hand suddenly stopped and clamped over her mouth.

"I would love to have a peek at the clothing shops." Ruby rolled down the window and breathed in the air. "I've heard they rival Paris."

Makeda wriggled in excitement next to her. "I adore perfume. Are we going to Paulo's shop first?"

They drew up alongside a cobblestone walkway, in front of a window filled with exquisite bottles of different sizes and colours. Paulo had already escorted the Princess, Florence, and Elke into the shop.

A wall of scent almost drove Fina back out into the street. Gardenias, roses and jasmine. At the counter, the Princess rubbed scent on her neck. She closed her eyes to breathe in the aroma, then swayed slightly. Gripping the counter, she made her way to a high-backed wicker chair in the corner, where she sat heavily, eyelids still half-closed.

As if compelled by one scent in particular, Ruby rushed over to a green bottle in the window. Makeda and Iveta chatted with Paulo. He grinned like a proud parent.

"Jeremy is a dear, isn't he, darling Paulo? He flies me everywhere."

The corners of Paulo's eyes tightened. "He is an accomplished pilot, yes. But sometimes he can be most difficult to persuade."

Florence, meanwhile, had moved past the mid-priced bottles of scent on the main shelf, straight to the smallest and most expensive bottles behind the counter. "I'd like to try that one, please." The clerk offered her the squat green-and-red bottle. With an expert and practised hand, Florence swiped the scent across her wrist.

She handed over a fat wad of escudos to the clerk. "I'll take that. As well as a bottle of your Tabu Divine."

Fina stood near the door, still overwhelmed by the wall of scent. Almost unconsciously, her eyes were drawn to Makeda's erratic movements. Peculiar. She was normally so graceful.

Fina blinked. Makeda slipped a small red bottle into her handbag.

Now on a mission, Fina rushed to Ruby. "Don't look now, but Makeda pilfered a perfume."

Ruby put a hand up to her mouth and covered it as she spoke. "Why would she need to do that? She has plenty of money."

"I haven't a clue, but let's watch her more closely."

Now in sleuthing mode, Fina leaned against the counter, giving her an excellent vantage point over the store, and most especially young Makeda.

Fina whispered to Florence, "Would you introduce me to the Princess?"

Florence set down a large bottle on the glass counter. "I'm so sorry, I meant to introduce you. She led Fina to the Princess's chair. "Princess Thalia, this is Fina Aubrey-Havelock."

"Pleased to meet you, Miss Aubrey-Havelock." The Princess held out a steady hand, even though her brown ringlets quivered. Was Fina supposed to kiss her hand? She was rescued by Ruby, who also received the royal introduction.

"Try this, Miss Dove," said the woman behind the counter, proffering a strip of paper to Ruby. The woman had light streaks of beautiful grey in her hair, and delicate long fingers.

Outside, Paulo paced back and forth in front of the window. A young boy dashed up to him and handed him a message, then scampered off again.

The door to the shop opened. Paulo's mouth was set in a grim line. "Miss Armitage and Your Highness. Please come with me. It's urgent for your safety that you leave. Now."

19

"Follow that car!"

Pixley chuckled. "I've always wanted to say that."

"This isn't a game, Pixley. It's serious," said Gayatri.

Pixley cupped his hand around his ear. "I recognise the voice of a big sister."

She smiled. "Perhaps. Sorry, I'm on edge. I didn't sleep well last night."

"Neither did I." He removed his spectacles and wiped his eyes with a handkerchief. "Where are they going to? I thought they were going east towards the university in Lisbon, but they're driving north."

The driver looked back at them. Gayatri nodded. The car sped up the winding hill behind the other car.

"It's fortunate we have a few cars in front of us. But I wonder how long we can remain unnoticed."

"That 'Salvador' chap and the Doutor are scarcely ones to notice much of anything." Gayatri glanced over the cliff and then quickly looked away. "Who you think murdered Hendrik?"

"If it was the roulette chip – as Ruby surmised – then it must be one of the guests around the roulette table. Though I suppose it might be the Princess or Miss Armitage, as they were both playing before it happened."

"What about motive?"

"I haven't a clue. If the Princess or Miss Fieraru had been murdered then it would be much easier to determine. What do we know about Hendrik?"

"An importer-exporter with Zuster chocolate. He seemed every inch the bourgeois businessman."

Pixley rubbed his chin. "And yet, he looked troubled. Something was weighing on his mind. Chocolate... You know, I read a cracking detective novel once, where someone was given a box of chocolates but each sweet had been injected with poison, and then sealed up again with melted chocolate, making the gift the perfect murder weapon. You don't think..."

"Pixley!" Gayatri rolled her eyes at him. Up ahead, their quarry still climbed the hill.

"All right, perhaps it's a bit far-fetched. In any case—"

Their car suddenly screeched to a halt.

The driver gripped the wheel and turned it to the left, onto a winding dirt road.

Another car followed behind them.

"Look!" Gayatri pointed at a sign half-covered in ivy. "It's a monastery."

"Why here? And why is another car following us?"

Gayatri twisted her plait in her fingers. "I'm doing my best not to be nervous. What's our plan of action when we arrive at the monastery?"

"Excellent question. I have no idea. I thought we would walk behind them at the university, with plenty of people about. But this place might be deserted."

Gayatri leaned forward and mumbled in Portuguese. She leaned back. "I told the driver to wait for us, no matter what. He must be our escape car."

"What, are you saying we'll follow them on foot – and somehow they won't notice?"

A sharp turn to the right startled them. The driver held up a hand as the car lumbered over several holes before coming to a halt in front of an ancient stone building covered in bright green moss.

Pointing at the pathway nearest them, the driver slid out of the car. Pixley and Gayatri alighted onto the soft mounds of dirt, which were covered in luscious vegetation.

"Let's do as the driver says and follow the pathway." Pixley hunched over as if the sky had suddenly lowered and he didn't want to bump his head. Gayatri led them down the winding path, amidst the cacophony of birdsong. They arrived at a knoll overlooking the area where the other cars had parked.

The driver of one car was leaning against the door, smoking a cigarette. There was no sign of the others.

"Shh..." Gayatri put a hand to her ear. "Can you hear voices?"

Pixley shook his head. "I'll follow you."

They moved out of sight and circled behind the monastery buildings. The Salvador imposter and Fausto came into view, walking side by side. Fausto leaned forward while 'Salvador' clasped his hands behind his back. The men walked past a fountain with a gargoyle leering at them. As they approached Gayatri and Pixley's hiding spot, their voices grew louder.

"Did she come through with the goods?"

"Yes. Though I hope she has the sense to keep her mouth shut." Fausto's deep baritone echoed across the rocks, despite the lush surroundings.

Salvador halted. "Do you have it with you?"

A dark green light flashed amidst the vegetation. The doctor held up an emerald the size of a robin's egg.

Salvador grinned. "I'll bank it. Just as soon as I'm sure I can do it without him knowing."

Pixley exchanged glances with Gayatri.

As she looked back at him, Gayatri lost her footing. A small avalanche of dirt tumbled off the overhang where they sat. Startled, Salvador and Fausto looked up. Gayatri and Pixley retreated into invisibility.

"What was that?" The man calling himself Salvador grabbed the jewel and tucked it away in his pocket.

"Relax," said Fausto. "It was just an animal."

Shoulders stiff, Salvador shook his head and hurried down the pathway.

A gruff voice rose up behind Gayatri and Pixley.

"And just what are you doing?"

20

The magic spell of the perfume shop vanished.

Paulo, Florence, and the Princess sped away in the waiting car. Iveta, Makeda, Elke, Ruby, and Fina looked at one another. Iveta shrugged. "We must continue to shop." She hooked her arm through Elke's and practically dragged her next-door.

Makeda smiled after her.

"Your mother is, well, rather stupendous, isn't she?" said Fina.

"She is a force of nature. I adore her, of course, though she is often carried away by the moment."

"What do you mean?" Ruby pushed open the shop door.

"Impulsive. And over-generous. She lives life to its fullest, which means sometimes she pays a heavy price."

Fina thought wryly of Makeda's impulsive theft of the perfume. Like mother, like daughter.

Makeda's cryptic observation was cut short by delighted squeals. Ruby rushed to a pebbly silk halter gown in red. The clothes were indeed the latest fashions.

Iveta brought a smile to Elke's face as she held up white silk pyjama trousers – truly her style.

Fina admired Elke's choice. "You have exquisite taste. Is that because you're a photographer?"

"How did you know that?" Elke's lips pursed.

Ruby rescued Fina. "Paulo told us about your Lisbon exhibition last year – when you first visited the hotel."

The rouged lips reappeared as Elke relaxed. "Yes. I believe most photographers have excellent taste. As I do—"

Fina squirmed inwardly at Elke's immodesty.

"—but they frequently do not care about their own aesthetics. I suppose I am an exception."

Elke turned her focus on a vermilion satin gown.

"May I try this on?" Fina held up a lustreless orchid crêpe frock to the shopkeeper.

The man's face contorted. His eyelid twitched. "This is not a *department* store, miss." He said the word *department* as if it were the name of a relative who had brought shame on a Victorian family. "We do, however, have a place where you may try on the gown." Fina and Elke followed him to the back of the shop. Elke had the satin gown in her hand.

Behind a large velvet curtain stood two stalls lined with curtains.

The shopkeeper held open the curtains for each of the women. Fina set down her bag on a stool and removed her clothes. The frock proved obstinate, however. At first, she stepped into it, but her hips did not cooperate. Then she slid the frock over her head and pulled it down. The front slid into place, but not the back. Drat. Must be caught on something. She twisted her arm behind her, trying to unhook the button. As she contorted her arm, she twisted her body around, pulling down on the dress. A sudden jerk told her of success, but also foretold disaster.

Fina tumbled over, pulling the curtains down with her. The entire contraption collapsed.

"What have you done?" screeched Elke, who stood in her underclothes. Her hands flew up to her neck and bosom.

The shopkeeper pulled back the curtain and then whirled around at the sight of the women in their underclothes. "Are you injured?" he asked over his shoulder.

"No," said Fina and Elke in unison.

Ruby slipped in past the shopkeeper and ran towards the heap of red curtains. Fina lifted herself onto her elbows and looked around in a daze. "So sorry, Elke. It was an accident."

While Ruby held up the curtains as a makeshift cover, Elke changed back into her clothes. All she said was, "Hmph."

The contents of Elke's bag lay scattered on the floor. Even in her bewildered state, Fina's eyes fixed on the objects as if they were diamonds in the rough.

Lipstick, rouge, notebook, pencil, sunglasses, a tin of soda mints, and three passports. One was in Dutch. One was in Cyrillic. And one was in English, but it wasn't a British passport.

Before Fina could help herself to the contents of the bag by offering to rearrange them, Elke scooped up the passports. As she did, a photograph fell out from between the pages of one of them. A man stood with his back to the camera. A flag hung on the wall with three horizontal stripes and a crest with an eagle, moon, sun, and castles.

As Ruby helped Fina to her feet, she whispered, "Did you spy those passports?"

Fina nodded as she slid her own frock over her head. She said to Elke, "You must have many family members scattered all over the globe."

Elke froze. She straightened up, throwing the rest of her belongings back into her umbrella handbag. Then a slow smile spread over her face, like honey spilled on a table-top.

"That's because I'm a secret agent."

Fina was speechless. Then Elke let out a throaty, deep laugh. "I was joking. Pulling the leg." She pointed a finger at Fina's face and then covered her mouth in another laugh. "If you could have seen your face – not Ruby's face – but your face, Fina."

Burying her face in her bag, Fina mumbled, "Ah yes, my mistake."

Unconcerned, Elke swept past them with a still-immaculate gown in her hand.

Fina held open the shop door for Ruby as they stepped into the bright sun.

"I wonder what those passports are about. Must be for Hendrik's import-export business." Ruby shielded her eyes from the sun. "Let's stroll a bit. I need to clear my head."

Fina nodded. "I'm a bit woozy from the scent and I have some questions as well. What was the danger to the Princess? And why has she seemed, well, as weak as an ailing chick?"

"Indeed. Though it's not just weakness. She's jumpy one minute and then in a dreamlike state in another." Ruby fell silent for a moment, then grabbed Fina's arm.

"Ow."

"So sorry, Feens. It's just that I remembered what happened at breakfast. Did you notice Florence giving the Princess pills at breakfast? Her hands were shaking."

Now Fina grabbed Ruby. "Florence's handbag spillage reminds me of last night. Pills fell out of her handbag last night when she was at the bar. I didn't think much of it at the time."

"Do you think the Princess is ill?" Ruby shook her head as if in answer to her own question. "Perhaps. But it's more than that. She might be ill, but her behaviour reminds me of Nelly. In college. Remember?"

"You mean Nosy Nelly? I had forgotten about her – so much has happened since my first year at Quenby. If I remember correctly, she said she'd been taking drugs to help her study, correct?"

Ruby twisted an earring. "Precisely. And it seems it did help her, for a time at least. But then she began to act oddly, not showing up to classes, and..."

Fina wrinkled her nose. "Oh yes! The smell! I remember now. Her hygiene routine became, well, non-existent."

"Do you think Florence is drugging the Princess?"

"But why?"

"I don't know. Money?"

"Did you notice Florence's expensive perfume tastes just now, in the shop?" asked Fina. "She not only forked over a great wad of cash, but did it with such nonchalance that it seemed as though it were an everyday occurrence."

"But how is drugging the Princess connected to her extra income?"

"Good question. Is stealing from her too obvious?"

Ruby tapped her teeth. "Florence seems too clever for such a simple scheme. Besides, someone would notice the absence of money at some point. What if someone is paying Florence to drug the Princess?

"To what end?"

Ruby sighed. "I haven't a clue." She looked at her wristwatch. "Jeremy said we ought to be at the hotel by two o'clock, if we want to go up in the aeroplane with him."

A wave of queasiness washed over Fina. "Yes, I suppose we ought to. The shops are spiffing, though. Perhaps we ought to take him up on it – no pun intended – tomorrow?"

"You can't fool me, Feens," giggled Ruby. "I know you don't enjoy flying. But the man is a decorated pilot – we'll be safe in his hands. And we might learn something."

"Where has this sudden rush of trust for fellow humans come from, I wonder?"

Ruby bent her head. "He is terribly handsome, isn't he?"

"Aha! I knew that was the reason. I agree, but what if he murdered poor Hendrik? We'll be in a plane piloted by a murderer!"

21

Gayatri and Pixley spun round.

The handsome face of Teodoro displayed a charming gap-toothed smile. But menace lurked behind the grin.

Pixley leaned against a rock and pulled himself up. "We were admiring the lovely garden below. Fantastic vantage point, what?"

Gayatri waved her hands. "I'll sketch it when we return to the hotel!"

Teodoro moved closer. So close. "I'm sure you've enjoyed the scenery. But you won't be returning to the hotel."

"What the devil?" Pixley flung out his arms and sucked in his gut, causing his enormous barrel chest to puff out.

Gayatri pushed past Teodoro. She stopped. Two men with sizeable bulk, straining muscles, and mouths grimly set blocked the pathway.

Teodoro smirked. "I see you've met Álvaro and Nilo. They're friends of mine who will see you to the car. Come along."

Pixley and Gayatri clambered into the back of Teodoro's car. A henchman gave Pixley an additional shove.

"I say! No need to push," squawked Pixley.

Teodoro turned round from the front seat. "I think we will do without the handcuffs, since you have proved obliging so far."

"Are you with the police?" Gayatri leaned forward.

"Quiet!" Teodoro yelled. Then his pleasant but menacing smile returned. "I'm sorry, but do not ask silly questions, Miss Badarur. I was about to say that while handcuffs are unnecessary, I'm afraid blindfolds are obligatory. For your own safety."

GAYATRI PACED BACK and forth across the uneven floorboards. "Where are we?"

Pixley peeked through the ragged chintz curtains adorning the one small window in the room. "I spy a few trees. Looks like a back garden in someone's house." He jiggled the handle on the window. "In case you're wondering, someone's painted the blasted window shut."

"It wouldn't have been much use, since we're on the first floor anyway. At least the smell of cooking – perhaps it's soup – makes me more at ease."

"It makes me queasy. The cosy atmosphere mixed with menace." Pixley leaned against the wall and then slid down until he came to rest on a crate.

"Why on earth would Teodoro want to keep us here?" Gayatri fumed. "He guards the Princess, but we had nothing to do with the Princess – we were watching two different people in a monastery on a hill, for pity's sake!"

"You're pacing like Ruby."

Gayatri flung back her plait behind her neck. "I know. I'm hoping I'll channel her smashing deductive skills. So far, it isn't working."

"You've got to make little circles," smiled Pixley. "You're walking straight back and forth."

Gayatri laughed. "If I had to choose someone to be cooped up like this with in danger, I'd choose you."

"Likewise." Pixley pulled his jacket a little closer. The temperature had dropped. "You're so calm. Unless you have a gleam in your eye while gambling."

"Ha! I plan to live to see that day again."

"You don't think they'll hurt us, do you?" Pixley shifted on the rickety crate.

The door opened.

A jolly, motherly woman entered with a tray of steaming broth, a plate of olives, bread, and cheese. And a pitcher of wine.

She smiled, bowed, and put the tray on a large crate. "*Obrigada. Bom apetite!*" She bowed again and scurried out, gently closing the door and turning the lock.

Pixley licked his lips. "Let's eat! I'm famished."

Gayatri put a hand on his arm. "Wait. What about poison?"

"What? That nice little old lady, poisoning us?"

Gayatri peered sceptically at the broth. She sniffed.

Pixley shrugged. "Think of it this way. If they wanted to kill us, they would have already. We must eat eventually. I'll be the official taste tester. If I die, you can tell the others what happened. I'd rather be poisoned than die another way."

Leaning over the food, Gayatri eyed it as if it were a medical experiment.

Pixley swiped a piece of bread, dunked it in the broth and stuffed it into his mouth. "Marvellous. Just marvellous," he said in between swallows. He poured a glass of wine, saluted Gayatri, and downed it in one gulp. "I love Portuguese wine," he sighed.

Gayatri tentatively fingered a piece of bread, first turning it over between her fingertips. Then she tore off a corner, slipped it into her mouth, and let it dissolve.

Pixley held up a spoon. "See? Nothing to worry about. Come on. It's delicious."

After the bread had fully dissolved, Gayatri dug into the meal with gusto. She sliced a large chunk of cheese, buried it in the warm bread and stuffed it into her mouth, all washed down with a large glass of white wine.

Soon, she was giggling. Pixley giggled too. In between giggles, Pixley said, "It must be the wine. Or shock."

He popped a few olives in his mouth and then, with total abandon, aimed his head towards the corner of the room. He spat the stones with surprising accuracy into the corner. Instead of pinging onto the floor, however, they disappeared.

Gayatri rose and crept over to the corner with Pixley close behind her. "Look!"

22

———

After a rapid change of clothes and a short ride to the airstrip, Fina and Ruby walked across the runway – a strip of green grass. The sea sparkled white and blue to the south – a sharp contrast to the brown, scrubby grass around the landing strip. No one else was in sight. Hairs prickled on her arms. "Where are Pixley and Gayatri? Weren't they supposed to meet us here?"

"Paulo said a phone call came in to say they had been unavoidably detained."

"I hope they've had more luck than we have, despite that intriguing passport incident with Elke. What did you make of it?"

Ruby tightened the belt on her trench coat. "If the Vogels are involved in the smugglers' ring, then multiple passports make sense. But the Russian and American passports bother me. Based on Idris's information, neither of those countries are on the smugglers' itinerary."

The silver nose on the aeroplane seemed to wink at Fina in the sun. She shivered.

"Jeremy's aeroplane is much larger than I'd pictured it," said Ruby. "That means it should be a smoother ride."

"He's a smooth one himself, that Jeremy," said Fina.

"He certainly looks like a film star."

"It's true, but it's more than that. I forgot to mention it before, but remember when we were in the hallway yesterday?"

"When Iveta cornered me?" laughed Ruby.

"Yes, well, right before that, Jeremy said he was from Cornwall. Intuitively, something seemed off. So I thought I'd give him a little test."

Ruby halted. "Fina Aubrey-Havelock. You're more devious than I'd ever imagined! Go on."

A little glow of pleasure relaxed Fina's rigid, nervous limbs. "I said that his tanned face made it look like he hadn't been cold as a jelis in a long time."

"Jupiter's teeth. What does that mean? Is it a Cornish saying?"

"The correct Cornish saying is 'cold as a quilkin'. Quilkin is a frog."

"So he's not from Cornwall?"

"Quite the contrary, my dear! Did you see his face? He looked bemused. If he was masquerading as a Cornishman, he would have gone along with it. No, I believe he's the genuine article."

Jeremy's head popped up from the aeroplane door. His white scarf rippled against a brown leather jacket. "So glad you're joining me. Smashing day, what? And not much wind."

Fina let out a tiny stream of air. Ruby patted her shoulder.

"But who knows what might occur once we're over the ocean."

Her stomach clenched.

"Just joshing, Fina," he said. "I hope I didn't upset you."

Ruby put an arm around Fina. "She's a nervous passenger. I have to admit I'm much the same."

Jeremy saluted them. "Orders received. I'll be as gentle as a lamb."

They clambered up the stairway and ducked into the aeroplane. Fina wrinkled her nose at the heady mixture of cologne, cigarette smoke, and leather. She stuck her head out and inhaled the sea air.

Something nipped at her heel. She looked down and spotted Cici inspecting her ankle. Then her eyes slewed to the right. Lena.

Lena slapped her thigh. "Ah, Cici loves pastries. Did you eat pastries this morning, Miss Aubrey-Havelock? You look like someone who enjoys her pastries."

Fina's muscles tightened as she spun round. "Why don't you say it? You think I'm fat?"

With a chuckle, Lena held up her hands in mock surrender. "My dear, you have a wonderfully curvy figure. Just like mine. Nothing to be ashamed of. Some men like that."

Ruby and Jeremy had slight grins on their faces. Fina was certain the temperature inside the cabin and her embarrassment must have turned her face beetroot-red. She slipped into the seat in front of Lena and next to the pilot. Perhaps sitting next to Jeremy would restore a sense of control.

Ruby eyed Cici. "Are dogs allowed?"

"Are you questioning my Cici?" Lena lifted herself out of the seat. Fina smiled at Ruby's jab.

Jeremy waved his hands gently downward, as if he were finishing a quiet piano piece. "Ladies, ladies, calm yourselves."

"What did you say?" Ruby spun round so quickly her skirts covered Cici in a flurry of blue voile.

Jeremy squinted as he puffed on a cigarette. "No need to be hysterical."

"We're grateful for your hospitality, Mr Salter, but please don't patronise us."

He sucked on his cigarette and then blew the smoke out of a corner of his mouth. "Mmmm... I like feisty women." Then he held up his hands. "Point taken, I'm sorry. Shall we get on with it?"

"Please," said Ruby. She sighed as she sat down across from Lena.

As the aeroplane taxied slowly, Fina turned to Jeremy. "Why did the police allow us to fly? Aren't they concerned we'll suddenly disappear?"

Jeremy flung his scarf across his neck. "I didn't tell them. Lena here joined me at the last minute. Only Paulo knows, so we haven't anything to worry about – we can beg forgiveness later."

Fina looked back at Ruby. Lips pursed, brow furrowed, she gripped the armrest as they gained speed. Fina mustered up the courage to give her a reassuring smile. Cici began to yap.

The aeroplane sped towards the sea. Though it was an optical illusion, the way the runway looked as though it plunged into the sea only made Fina clench her jaw tighter. Suddenly, they lifted up, like a bird in shifting winds.

"Will you tell your little dog to shut up?" cried Ruby over the hum of the engine.

Fina turned her head so quickly she winced at her pulled neck muscle. Ruby's head had disappeared between her knees. "Shall we turn back, Ruby?"

Ruby groaned. "No, I'll be fine. If that blasted dog is quiet."

Leaving one hand on the yoke, Jeremy motioned to a box near Fina. "There are bits of dried meat in there for emergencies. Would you give them to Cici?"

The hard brown bits soon quieted the little beast. Lena's coos over the dog interrupted the engine's white noise.

In an effort to distract Ruby from an increased murderous intent against Cici, Fina pointed at the window. "Isn't it beautiful?"

Zipping along the shoreline, the aeroplane passed over enormous cliffs plunging into a variegated blue sea. Small clusters of houses interspersed with larger villages dotted the cliffs.

Fina's declaration only received approval from Jeremy. "It's grand, isn't it? I'm free as a bird up here. It's my favourite place to be."

"Other than home in Cornwall?" Fina brushed off an errant bit of dried meat from her lap.

"Ah, Cornwall. It has its troubles, but for natural beauty, you can't top it anywhere in the world."

"Do you fly only for yourself? Were you ever in the RAF? Or flown for a commercial airline?"

The aeroplane dipped and then evened out, gently flipping Fina's stomach. "I trained as an RAF pilot at the tail-end of the Great War, but then had an honourable discharge." He grimaced.

"And how about for these commercial airlines? Do they pay well?"

"Some of them do. I did a year-long stint, but soon became restless. I'm a wandering chap." He winked at Fina. "It's terribly boring flying back and forth to the same place, day after day."

Fina thought it anything but boring to feel one was going to die every day, but she remained silent. They made a sharp left turn. Chatting with Jeremy helped keep her fear at bay, so she continued.

"So you fly now simply for pleasure?"

Long fingernails brushed against the back of Fina's neck. Lena leaned forward. "Darling Jeremy flies me around, yes, don't you?"

Jeremy's knuckles turned white. "Yes, I've flown most of the guests at the hotel – at least the ones present at the tragedy last night. They pay well. Paulo and I have an arrangement."

"Yes, we pay well." Cici yapped in support of Lena's declaration. "It's worth a little money for the enormous convenience."

"Is there anyone you haven't flown among the guests?"

"Ah, Salvador Carvalho, for one. He's a new arrival – I'd never met him until a few days ago. But most of the others are regulars. I've even flown Paulo to Amsterdam."

"I wonder why the Vogels and the Princess arrived via ship, then."

They jerked to the right. "I'm not sure about the Vogels, but the Princess avoids flying whenever possible. She does not like it. Florence told me she's rather nervy in general."

Lena leaned forward. "The Princess is a coward."

Ruby's face reappeared. "That's rather rude."

Unconcerned by Ruby's challenge, Lena replied, "But it's true. She avoids me and runs away like a mouse every time I appear. Last night, she ran away after I arrived at the roulette table. A true princess does not run away, even if she is nervous."

Ruby was in a foul temper. "I wouldn't wish to be around my husband's mistress, either."

Though Fina could not fully turn around, her seat rocked, presumably due to Lena's quivering body.

Fina intervened before a small scuffle broke out behind her. "What do you think happened last night?"

Jeremy opened his mouth but Lena's words streamed forth like a gushing river. "I cannot understand it. Why would that poor man commit suicide? And like that? If I were to kill myself, it would be quick. A revolver or pills, I think," she said as if she were perusing the latest fashions in Estoril. "I dislike these events. There is something evil at the hotel."

"Did you know the Vogels?" asked Ruby.

"I know them as one does at these resorts. In Monte, too, of course. You see them season after season, and nod politely."

"I stood near the Vogels at one point during the roulette

play." Jeremy wiped his forehead with a handkerchief. "And I didn't notice Hendrik putting anything on his chips – nor anyone else, either."

"Did you know them well?" asked Fina.

"Like Lena, I knew them on a surface level. I flew them once from Amsterdam to Berlin. And once from Amsterdam to Rome. Hendrik was a fine fellow, though his wife kept him under her thumb. They make excellent chocolate."

Fina's stomach rumbled.

"Was that thunder? We're going to die!" Lena bounced up and down. "Thunder and lightning!"

Jeremy chuckled. "No need to worry, Lena. I think it was a false alarm." He grinned at Fina. Fina suddenly became fascinated by the shoreline.

"Speaking of chocolate." Ruby leaned forward and put a hand on Jeremy's seat. "Do you ever fly things other than people, like chocolate or perfume – or even precious stones – to various places? Such as—"

Her words died away as the aeroplane's nose jerked downwards.

23

Gayatri and Pixley peered downwards. The floor had rotted through, creating a peephole into the world below.

"Sounds like Romanian," said Gayatri. "And Portuguese. And another language I don't recognise."

Teodoro and the friendly cook moved around the table. The cook served the henchmen steaming bowls of soup while Teodoro circled the table, smoking a cigarette.

A henchman banged on the table. He pointed upwards, towards Gayatri and Pixley's room. Teodoro nodded and disappeared.

The door flew open. Teodoro's arms were folded close against a suit spotted with dust. He grabbed a chair from the corridor and sat on it backwards.

Pixley and Gayatri stood in the corner, as stuck as limpets to a rock.

"You've found the hole in the floor. Excellent. I assumed you would." Teodoro held out a packet of cigarettes. "Would you like one?"

Still frozen in place, Pixley and Gayatri shook their heads in unison.

"Please, make yourselves at home. I won't bite." He swept a hand around the room as if he were showing them his grand palace.

They lowered themselves onto the crates.

"I see you've enjoyed your meal. Mama Corbu is a splendid cook, isn't she?"

Silence.

Teodoro puffed on his cigarette and then stared at it as if it were an unknown object. "It's time to tell you why you are my honoured guests. I don't want to keep you too long as I'm sure your charming friends will search for you soon – or worse, alert the police."

Pixley cleared his throat. "We meant no harm. We were simply following Fausto and, er, Salvador."

Gayatri gave Pixley a venomous glance and crossed her arms.

"Miss Badarur does not approve of your confession, but I assure you it's the correct thing to do." He flicked a bit of tobacco away from his lips. "As a goodwill gesture, I'll tell you we've no interest in you, but we need to understand why you followed Senhor Carvalho and Doutor Tavares."

Pixley looked at Gayatri. She shrugged. "We are watching a ring of thieves who smuggle items around Europe."

Teodoro's eyes narrowed. Gayatri turned towards Pixley.

"We overheard Salvador and Fausto discussing precious stones, so we assumed they must be part of the ring." Pixley sighed. "Why were *you* following them?"

Teodoro waved his cigarette. "We're also interested in the gems, but not for the same reasons. Do you know an Idris Maghur, by chance?"

Gayatri and Pixley shifted on their rickety crates.

"I see that you do." Teodoro smiled. "That is a relief. We're not exactly in the same game, but you might say we have a few common interests. Are you familiar with the plight of the Roma?"

Pixley pushed his spectacles further up his nose, "Oh, yes. Simply dreadful – do you work for them? Is there a campaign?"

Teodoro coughed and nodded, suddenly looking frail. "Yes, my family are Roma and we would like better conditions in Romania. While Charles II does not target us in the way other regimes have, we are invisible."

Gayatri's eyes widened. "You don't have plans to assassinate the Princess, do you?"

This time Teodoro's cough was combined with a laugh. "Oh no, not that at all." He smiled. "Though if we did, I'd scarcely tell you. No, if we were to attempt something, we would suffer the King's terrible retribution. We're trying a more gentle, persuasive approach. But to be successful, we need access to the King, and money."

Pixley's leg jiggled. "So you gain access to the King by persuading his wife. And you gain money by stealing the jewels from this smuggling ring."

"I prefer to say we're redistributing the jewels. These wealthy people don't need another diamond on their necklace. Or emerald."

The door opened, revealing a bulldog-faced henchman. He and Teodoro had a rapid-fire exchange in an unknown language. Teodoro turned back to them. "He wants to know what he should do with you."

24

———

Fina's hands moulded themselves around the armrests of her seat. Her stomach clenched. Her entire body clenched.

Was something burning? Why was it so quiet?

Breathe, Fina, breathe.

She closed her eyes.

The aeroplane continued its rapid descent.

"Is there a reason we're descending so quickly?" Ruby's muffled voice came from the back seat.

"We've lost power. We may need to make a dead stick landing. I'm working on it. Half a mo."

Dead stick. Not words Fina wanted to hear. Despite the voices in her head screaming at her to keep her eyes shut, Fina peeled back one eyelid and squinted.

Jeremy was calmly fiddling with dials and switches. But beads of sweat trickled down his forehead.

Lena screamed. Then she mumbled what sounded like a prayer.

Cici barked. Lena must have smothered the poor dog because the barking stopped as rapidly as it had begun.

The blue of the sea came closer and closer.

A definite burning smell.

"Aha!" Jeremy flicked a switch in triumph. "All fixed now."

"Why are we still going down, then?" Ruby asked. Fina had tried to ask these questions but her vocal cords had ceased working.

"Wait..." He held up a hand. "There."

The aeroplane's nose gradually lifted, until they were horizontal again.

Though her body was still frozen from the adrenaline, Fina mopped her whole face with her handkerchief, as if she were removing cold cream.

"*Dumnezeule*, my God," said Lena.

"Indeed," echoed Ruby.

Jeremy's fingers shook as he shifted the gears once more. He gave out a little jangling laugh. "So sorry about that. Looks as though something went wrong with the power. Which is odd, because I checked everything last week."

"Do you think a part was faulty?" asked Fina.

"Couldn't be. I flew at least three times last week and everything was smooth as silk."

"Are you saying someone tampered with it?"

"That's the only plausible explanation. Do you have other ideas?"

"Tea would be wonderful. And a pastry, please. *Pastel de Nata*?"

The waiter nodded. Fina smiled back, her mouth watering in anticipation of the glorious pastry.

Ruby set down her menu and shook her head at the waiter. "Glad you can eat again." She held her stomach. "I'm still queasy."

"Ginger tea. That will do the trick." Fina waved the waiter back and placed the order.

"Thank you, Feens. You're right. Ginger tea will help – holding something warm in my hands will stop the shaking."

Fina surveyed the hotel terrace. Except for a few guests scattered near the entrance, they were alone. The waves lapped quietly and a cool breeze ruffled her hair. She and Ruby, shivering from shock, had donned many layers of clothing upon returning to the hotel. They looked like two bundled-up grannies on the pier at Brighton.

A long stream of air from Ruby followed the breeze. "I'm ready to talk now. Tell me what you made of our dance with death – especially since you had an even better view of our impending doom from the seat next to Jeremy."

"Well, it was peculiar that the piffle-valve malfunction or whatever it was called—"

Ruby giggled uncontrollably. "Don't mind me. Your piffle-valve struck me as hilarious."

"Glad I can still make you laugh at a time like this." She cupped her hands around the warm cup of tea the waiter had brought. Eyeing the pastry, she suddenly broke her stare with the yellow eye in the centre of it and gazed at the sea. "I think the timing was odd. Just when we were asking him a thorny question."

"But did he have to be so dramatic about it?" Ruby sipped her ginger tea and smiled. "Couldn't he have dodged our question rather than endangering us all?"

"I suppose. But perhaps it was a warning that he has complete freedom to do whatever he pleased?"

Ruby nodded. "It's a plausible supposition. It's also possible he was telling the truth and someone tampered with the so-called piffle valve."

"Such as?"

"For starters, there's the murderously batty cove who placed a knife in a melon next to your bed this morning!"

"I forgot about that temporarily. Almost dying in an aeroplane crash will do that."

"Assuming it wasn't our mysterious visitor and that Jeremy is hiding something, it means he's at the centre of the smuggling operation. He must be the one who takes whatever they're moving around back and forth to various countries."

"I think it's a reasonable assumption. What about Lena? She strikes me as important, though I cannot put my finger on why it seems to be the case."

Ruby nodded. "Lena seems nervous. No. That's not it. She seems discontented."

"Discontented that she isn't married to the King, rather than the Princess?"

"Yes ... it makes me wonder about our drug-addled princess. Besides Florence and Teodoro, the only close connection to the Princess is Lena."

A clock chime echoed four times in the distance.

Fina confirmed the time on her wristwatch. "Where are those two? They were supposed to meet us an hour ago."

25

Ruby tilted her head to one side. "Your jaw is clenched. What's wrong?"

"I'm not sure. My magnetism is acting up, so perhaps a storm is brewing." Fina shivered, even though the sky was blue.

The waves lapped along the shore, adding to the veneer of calm. Ruby jumped out of her seat. "I'm too restless for a nap."

"Let's take a walk, shall we? It will clear our heads."

After a stroll through the trimmed gardens, they removed their shoes and stockings and set off along the shore.

"Ahh! It's cold!" Ruby hopped up and down.

"If we walk fast, we'll warm up." Fina pulled her coat closer. She wiggled her toes in the beige sand. As long as she didn't dig her toes in too deep, she'd stay warm.

The pair skipped above the wet shoreline, heading towards Lisbon. The smell of the sea mixed with wood smoke from a fire nearby. A group of men sat huddled around a grill laden with fish. Sardines.

"The walk was an excellent idea. I feel so much better now we're away from the hotel." Swinging her shoes, Ruby danced merrily towards the water.

"What are you doing? You'll catch your death if you go in there!" Fina's mother's voice had suddenly gripped her vocal cords.

"I dare you, Feens! It's not too cold!" Ruby twirled in the inch of water lapping against the shore.

Fina crossed her arms.

"Don't be a fusspot. Join me!"

Arms uncrossed, Fina shrugged and ran towards the waves. Her timing left something to be desired, however, as the water swelled and rolled over her legs, up to her knees.

Fina screeched so loudly that the men grilling fish turned their heads.

Laughing uncontrollably, Ruby took Fina's shoes and stockings and helped her away from the waves.

"Oh, I'm so sorry. Your frock is soaked!"

Fina grimaced. "Yes, I can see that. Thanks for nothing."

"No need to be cross. You'll dry off. We'll get you into new clothes."

Fina stamped her foot. As soon as she did, she realised what a childish gesture it was. "Fine. I'm too invigorated by our walk."

Her face turned hot as she walked past the men, who laughed and shook their heads.

As if she could read her mind, Ruby said, "I expect they're accustomed to tourists as foolish as a cow's calf. Don't worry – we've satisfied them by playing our expected role."

They sat down on steps near the beach and slipped on their shoes, without their stockings. Ruby said, "A penny for your thoughts. About the murder and our mission."

"I'm muddled about it all at the moment. What's odd is everyone had opportunity. At least, anyone around the roulette table could have doctored those chips. Elke wasn't there, and Teodoro was busy taking bets, of course. Could one arrange a murder with one hand while spinning a roulette wheel with the other? It would require fabulous feats of dexterity." She sighed. "Besides, everyone has the same motive."

"You mean they're somehow connected to this smuggling ring?"

"Precisely." Fina stopped to empty sand from her shoe. "Normally, we'd have suspects with opportunity and others with motives. But here, no one seems to have a specific reason to kill Hendrik."

"Yes..." Ruby paused. "And because they're all presumably part of the smuggling ring, they've reasons to act suspiciously."

"That's it. Maybe we should look for a suspect who acts normally. But that's rubbish, isn't it?"

"On the contrary, Feens. On the contrary. Brilliant deduction. We should pay attention to suspects who act unsuspiciously. Though one thing still bothers me about this morning."

"What's that?"

"The idea that Idris – or another person in the police force – told Cardoso about us." Ruby tapped her teeth.

"Speaking of Idris, have you seen him since he left us yesterday?"

Someone tapped Fina on the shoulder.

"Are you taking my name in vain?"

Fina flung her arms around Idris.

"Well, well. I ought to disappear more often." He wore a rolled-up, open-necked blue dress-shirt, with navy braces.

Two figures drifted into view from behind him. "Shall we leave you two alone?" Pixley grinned. Gayatri shivered but managed a smile.

"Pix! Gayatri!" Ruby embraced them both. "Where have you been?"

"We'll tell you all about it. After a nap." Gayatri stretched.

Pixley slapped Idris on the back. "This chap rescued us. He

has ties with Teodoro and his operation, so he came to fetch us from Teodoro's Lisbon hideaway."

Ruby's eyes widened. "Are you saying Teodoro kidnapped you?"

Gayatri pulled at her ear. "In a manner of speaking, yes. After we followed 'Salvador' and Fausto to the monastery, where they exchanged an emerald."

Fina turned to Gayatri. "Monastery? Emerald? What in blue blazes are you talking about?"

"Come on." Pixley waved at the hotel. Lena and Florence were chatting in the garden. "Let's have tea. We can swap stories and then have a nap."

"Don't sleep too long," said Idris. "Remember, tonight is New Year's Eve. And we have a grape celebration."

"A grape celebration?" Pixley rubbed at his eyes.

"Yes. I believe the hotel manager has arranged some sort of treasure hunt, with the celebration as a prize. As much as you deserve a long rest, we have work to do. All the guests will be assembled for the party tonight. And you must be on guard." Idris' delicate hands pantomimed their instructions.

"What should we be on guard for?" Gayatri asked.

"The murderer. And whoever else might be about. Your dossiers, remember?"

Gayatri looked away.

Ruby surveyed Idris. "Speaking of dossiers – and the police – did you tell the police about us?"

The smile on his face looped downward into a frown. "What do you mean?"

"Perhaps you told the police about us so they'd take us seriously when we began sleuthing."

Idris blinked. "I assure you, dear Ruby, I would do nothing of the sort. I'm not an intelligence agent, and I'd certainly never give the police any information about you." His voice wavered.

"I'm sure we're mistaken," said Fina. "The Comissário told us that a colleague told him about our past escapades. The only explanation was that you told them. Who else would know we're in Portugal?"

Pixley sighed. "Who indeed?"

"Please forgive me, Ruby. I thought you were questioning my loyalty." Idris spread out his hands. "But it seems we have someone else to reckon with."

26

———

Fina threw off the bedclothes. Despite overwhelming fatigue, her mind raced. She stared at the large crack on the ceiling, which resembled a rupture on a frozen pond. The two cracks joined into a triangular formation. She had seen something like that recently. But where?

She reached for the drawer in the bedside table. The note attached to the dreadful melon had vanished. Her heart pounded but slowed when she realised a maid had tidied the room.

Perhaps she had stuffed it into her coat pocket. As she slid off the bed and padded towards her coat, voices floated in from the hallway.

With her ear pressed against the door, Fina listened.

"You fool. Everything is ruined. That gang of young people – ruffians from London – are meddling in our affairs. And it's your fault," said Iveta, in an uncharacteristically monotone voice.

"My fault? My fault that Hendrik was murdered? And as for those young people – ruffians, as you call them – I can't be responsible for them. I'm sure I've led them up the garden path. But they're smart. Especially that Caribbean woman," said Elke.

A loud "tsk" echoed in the corridor. "She's British."

"What difference does it make? We are in the soup and all you care about is someone's nationality."

The voices faded away. Fina found the note in her coat pocket, along with a pen. She scribbled on the back of the ghastly warning note. Although she had a photographic memory, she had trouble remembering conversations. And therefore occasionally embellished stories.

The warning note confirmed Fina's memory. Someone had scrawled a tiny trapezoid in the bottom right-hand corner. It could be a poorly drawn diamond. A diamond would surely make more sense.

The grandfather clock ticked incessantly. Half past six. Ruby had had enough time to sleep. Fina tapped on her door, but there was no answer.

She tried Pixley. The door opened almost immediately. Already adorable in striped pyjamas, he had unwittingly amplified the effect with a tiny sleeping cap.

Barefaced and without spectacles, Pixley blinked at Fina as if she were the sun. "What is it?"

Fina handed him the note. "Read both sides."

"You'd better come in. I've misplaced my spectacles."

Fina ambled to a comfortable plush green chair.

"Pixley?" Gayatri's voice came through the adjoining door.

He lumbered towards the door. "Coming," he mumbled.

"Oh, hullo Fina. Trouble sleeping?"

Fina nodded.

"I couldn't either, so I caught up on correspondence. See what I found." Gayatri held up a crumpled piece of paper.

"Go on. You haven't received a threatening note yet, have you?"

"You make it sound like an everyday occurrence." Gayatri handed her the note.

"By Jove, it's becoming just that." Pixley held up another crumpled note. "This was underneath my spectacles on the desk." He dropped it like a hot potato. "Ah! Someone entered my room while I was napping!"

Gayatri picked up the note. "Yours is like mine – blank except for a trapezoid. But yours looks more like a diamond." She handed Pixley's note to Fina.

"What have I missed?" Ruby padded in from the doorway.

"A bit of excitement, as per usual." Fina handed Ruby the three notes.

"It's hard to tell if it's the same handwriting, since only one note has script. But could it be two different poison pens?"

"Unlikely, I'd say," said Pixley in his best serious-journalist voice.

"Excellent deduction, Sherlock," said Gayatri.

Pixley giggled and held up a hand. "Sorry. I know this is serious." He flung out his hands towards the notes. "But these notes are childish."

"A knife sticking out of a melon next to my bed is scarcely childish, Pix," Fina grumbled.

Ruby sat down on Pixley's bed. "So what do we make of this? Is it relevant to the murder? And watching the smuggling ring?"

Fina shrugged. "I'm not sure why, but they seem separate. There's something else going on here." She told them about what Elke and Iveta had been saying in the corridor.

"If they are separate, that's a whopping great coincidence, Feens," said Pixley.

"I agree, but something's different about these notes. More menacing."

"More menacing than murder?" asked Gayatri.

"I see where you're going, Feens," said Ruby. "A murderer is honest. No. That's not the correct word. But let's say a murderer takes action. Whereas this poison pen isn't actually doing anything."

"Nor do they give us instructions," said Gayatri. "It's almost as if they enjoy tormenting us."

"Precisely," said Ruby. "That's why the threats and the murder might be unrelated."

"So we ought to focus on discovery of the murderer's identity in a more conventional way," said Pixley.

"Yes. Especially given Iveta and Elke's conversation that Fina overheard. We must be on guard – remember Idris' warning."

"Well, it will be dashed difficult." Pixley shook his head.

"Why?" asked Gayatri. "Aren't we just having these grape festivities? It sounds like a regular party with the addition of a ceremony."

"That's true," said Pixley. "But Paulo said we'll have a treasure hunt before the grape festivities. How will we keep an eye on everyone when they're all split up?"

Gayatri clapped her hands. "A treasure hunt! But I adore treasure hunts!"

Although this girlish enthusiasm did not fit Gayatri's usual countenance, it did match her enthusiasm for games.

"I enjoy them, too," smiled Ruby. "Because I always win."

Pixley sat up straight and adjusted his spectacles. "Are you issuing a challenge, Miss Dove?"

"I assure you, Mr Hayford, it is exactly that."

"You know I cannot resist a challenge—"

"That's why I made it. And I will win. Or I should say, my team will win. I think we'll call ourselves the Sharp-Eyed Doves."

Their banter was interrupted by a paper slithering under the door.

27

Ruby groaned as Pixley fetched the folded paper. "Not another trapezoid, I hope."

Pixley mumbled, reading the note to himself. He looked up and smiled. "No need for concern. It's Paulo's treasure hunt instructions. How thoughtful." Pixley looked at his wristwatch. "The games begin in a half-hour."

Fina gripped the armrest. "But when will we have dinner?"

"The note says we'll have supper and festivities in the drawing room – then he'll announce the winner. The festivities will bring us into the new year."

Ruby looked at Fina as if she were a terminal patient. "We'd better figure out a way to refuel before the hunt begins. Especially if Fina is on my team."

"Does Paulo explain the teams?"

Pixley consulted the paper. "There are two teams. Funnily enough, it looks as though Idris helped plan the teams."

"Why's that?" asked Ruby as she hunted around in her bag.

"Because the teams roughly correspond to our dossier lists."

"Aha!" Ruby held up a packet of biscuits that read 'Bourbon'.

Pixley's tongue ran across his lips. "What are bourbons?"

"Creolas, naturally," said Fina as if he were as silly as a hen. "My favourite!"

Holding the biscuits aloft, as if a pack of hungry dogs surrounded her, Ruby said, "Whoever is on my team will receive an extra biscuit ration."

Gayatri snatched the note from Pixley. "Here's the list. That's rather adorable of Paulo. He named the teams after famous Portuguese pastries."

"Is he trying to torture us before dinner?" asked Fina.

"I think you're giving Paulo a little too much credit," said Pixley. "He's as fond of pastries as I am." Pixley patted his round belly.

"Well, I hope I'm on the *Pastel de Nata* team," said Fina.

"What does it mean?" asked Gayatri.

"Yummy. Custard cream," said Pixley.

"May we proceed with the teams?" Ruby let out a sigh of exasperation.

Fina giggled. "Look at Ruby's competitive streak. But I agree, let's push on, shall we?"

Gayatri nodded. "Team *Papos de Anjo*—"

"Angel's Double Chin!" cried Pixley. He put a hand over his mouth. "Sorry. Do go on."

"Angel's Double Chin is Gayatri, Ruby, Elke, Jeremy, Iveta, Florence, and the Princess."

Gayatri held out her hand to Ruby. "My extra rations, please."

Fina watched the chocolate cream sandwich biscuits pass before her eyes. With a laugh, Gayatri gave Fina half of her ration.

"So generous of you," said Fina.

"Now see what you've done," chuckled Ruby. "You've provided more fuel for the opposing team!"

"Very funny, Ruby," said Fina. "But it doesn't matter. Pixley and I – plus Lena, Makeda, 'Salvador', and Fausto will find the treasure so quickly we'll eat all of the supper before you arrive!"

"Right, Feens. Our team has personalities of steel." Pixley winked at Ruby and Gayatri. "Your team members are idle as a piper's little finger."

"We'll see about that," said Gayatri. "Our team has the famous Miss Ruby Dove."

The grandfather clock struck eight o'clock.

Ruby sprang up, swallowing the last of her bourbon biscuit. "Lord, we must fly if we don't want to disappoint our teams!"

THE DINING ROOM crackled with electricity. Sure enough, Fina looked down and saw her arm hairs standing on end.

Paulo addressed the crowd. "Ladies and gentlemen. I'm sure you're all excited about the treasure hunt. Unfortunately, a thunderstorm is approaching. Please be extra careful when searching outside. A few clues will lead you outside, but not too far from the hotel."

The crowd nodded, hanging on his every word. Only the Princess appeared nonplussed, as she absentmindedly flipped over a fork. Fina wondered why the Princess had decided to play at all. Teodoro stood near her, an unlit cigarette hanging from his lips.

"Get on with it, Paulo," growled Lena. Fina recognised a fellow sufferer of food-fatigue when she saw one – Lena's hands fidgeted and she scanned the room as if a plate of sandwiches might appear. Though Fina found Lena intimidating, she hoped her hunger would drive her to a win for their team.

"Right, Miss Fieraru." Paulo took out two envelopes with a flourish. He handed the first one to the Princess. She received it as if it were a letter of dubious origin.

Lena snorted. "Why does she get the envelope? Because she's a princess?"

Fina thought it as good a reason as any, from Paulo's point of view.

He bowed in Lena's direction. "No, my dear. I selected the team leaders at random." He gave Fausto the second envelope. Fausto bowed and received it as if it were a sacred chalice.

Paulo steepled his fingers. "When I give the signal, you may open your envelopes."

A hush fell over the room. Fausto gripped a pencil between his lips, ready to spring into action with both of his hands. In the corner, Jeremy blew insouciant smoke rings, though his twitching eyelid belied his casual stance. Elke sat on the edge of a table, swinging her signature silk-pyjama legs like a small child. Odd. She looked unbothered by her husband's death. Perhaps it was shock. In the seat next to Elke sat Lena, who had opted for the brightest red lipstick Fina had ever seen. Though it became Lena, it seemed a challenge to the Princess's faint, dusty rose lips. Lena clutched her evening bag as if Elke had threatened to snatch it away.

The Princess sat near the French windows in a fabulous blue gown, looking sullen. Though she had impeccable posture, it looked as if someone had stacked a group of soft coats onto a straight coatrack. Florence stood behind her, her white-gloved hand gripping the chair. A slight smile of anticipation illuminated her face. Fina goggled at the brooch on her collar. Surely she would have noticed it before. The gold brooch held a fantastic blue sapphire. Fina looked at Ruby and nodded in Florence's direction. Ruby's eyes widened and she nodded, signalling the brooch was a surprise to her.

Iveta and Makeda sat with the Princess. Makeda played with her emerald earrings, twisting them around and around, as if she were opening a jar. Clad in a white brocade gown with a matching cape and upswept hair, Iveta vied with the Princess for most glamorous. She drummed her fingers impatiently.

"Dear Paulo. Enough of the drama. Please let us begin." Iveta held out a hand as if she were directing a play.

Fausto tore his envelope open. The Princess handed hers to Florence. With one deft movement, Florence pulled a gleaming letter-knife from her handbag and sliced open the envelope.

28

―――――

Paulo's shiny, balding head nodded. He simpered and pulled his tie. "It's now half past eight. We gather at ten o'clock in the dining room. Whoever returns first with the treasure will be the winning team. And the person who solved the final clue on that team will receive the prize: a portion of the famous Muscat grapes, whose delicate flavour is much celebrated in our region, and indeed around the world."

"Does each team have the same clues?" asked Gayatri.

Paulo wagged his finger. "No, no. Otherwise, you would all follow one another. Too many opportunities for sabotage." He stood up straight. "You have separate clues. My staff and I have ensured that both sets are equally puzzling."

"What happens if neither team finds the treasure?" asked Pixley.

"In that case, whoever is farthest along will be the winner."

Pixley and Fina crowded around Fausto with Salvador, Makeda, and Lena close behind. Fausto cleared his throat. "The first clue is:

'Tis true I have both face and hands,
And move before your eyes,

Yet when I go, my body stands,
And when I stand, I lie."

Ruby's skirts brushed behind them as the other team rushed into the corridor. Iveta shrieked in excitement and delight.

Lena pounded the table. "I cannot concentrate with that woman squawking."

Makeda spun round while maintaining a regal bearing. "You're the one who squawks all the time. Not my mother."

Pixley held up one finger, as if to beg for silence. The gesture distracted Makeda and Lena. He closed his eyes and repeated the clue. "Face and hands."

"I'll tell you who it is," continued Lena as if she hadn't heard Pixley's plea. "I know someone who lies when they stand. The Princess!"

Makeda bleated a high, not unpleasing laugh.

The man calling himself Salvador sighed. He smiled at Pixley. "Any joy?"

Clapping his hands, Pixley said, "Yes! It's a clock. It has a face and hands. The hands move around. And when it stays still, it's lying – giving the wrong time."

Fausto slapped Pixley on the back. "Good man."

"But the hotel must have hundreds of clocks," said Salvador. "Which one is it?"

"It must be in the shared rooms," said Fina. "Might be a grandfather clock, since it mentions standing. Why don't we split up and search on the ground floor?"

"Excellent, Feens," said Pixley. "I'll go with the good Doutor."

Salvador rushed towards Fina. "We'll be a team." Fina felt her face flush.

Fausto studied the sulking Lena. "And Lena will join us."

Before Lena could say anything, Salvador grabbed Fina's hand and pulled her towards the library. His touch was surprisingly gentle. Once among the bookshelves, she closed her eyes and revelled in the silence for a moment.

"Are you ill?" He peered at her as her eyes opened.

"Oh, no. Overstimulated, that's all." She smiled. The man had a pleasing baby face.

Remembering they were not only on a treasure hunt, but a mission to discover more about the smuggling ring, she decided this was the perfect time to find out who he really was. "Have you enjoyed Estoril?" she asked, trying to sound casual. "Is this your first time here?"

His left hand quivered as he pulled it down from the wall clock. "Oh. Yes. It's my first time at this hotel, but not in Lisbon. I've visited Lisbon on business before."

"But I thought you were a historian. What kind of business?"

"Surely Gayatri has told you about it, since she seems to be the only one who has heard of me." He puffed out his chest, in a rare display of pride.

Fina decided to play along. "I know you oppose the Salazar regime and its colonial policies. That's most of what I know."

His back snapped upright, as stiff as a willow rod. "Absolutely abhorrent little man. He's an economist but he hasn't a clue about how economies run. If he pushes the colonies too far, they'll rebel and he'll have a costly war on his hands."

"Are you saying Goa will seek independence from Portugal?"

"In a word, yes. Though it may take a long time."

Fina leaned against a bookshelf. He certainly seemed sincere. "How will you fund the independence movement?"

Light danced on his spectacles, obscuring his eyes as he spoke. "You are clever. I've heard about you."

Glad of the support of the bookshelf, Fina tried her best nonchalant tone. "Oh, me? I'm not so clever. Ruby is the clever one."

A smile spread across his face. He moved a little closer.

Disconcerted by her inability to understand the smile, Fina scanned the room in the hope someone might be slumbering in a high-backed armchair.

The library was quiet. Too quiet.

Lena's head popped round the doorframe. For once, Fina was actually happy to see her.

She held up a scrap of paper. "We've found it! Come quickly so we can find the next clue!"

29

In the dining room, Florence, clutching her team's first clue in her gloved hand, cleared her throat as if she were about to sing. She intoned:

"*What force and strength cannot get through*
I with a gentle touch can do;
And many in the streets would stand,
Were I not, as friend, at hand."

Iveta's sleeves billowed as she made a dramatic gesture. "It must be ... a woman!"

Elke frowned. "How can a woman be a clue?"

Jeremy laughed. "I'm not sure about the gentle touch of a woman."

Gayatri punched Jeremy in the arm. Startled, he rubbed the spot. After a moment's pause, he gave an uneasy chuckle and glanced at the Princess. "Excuse me, Your Highness. No offence taken, I hope."

She eyed Jeremy as if she had seen him for the first time and waved him away.

"Why is our team larger than the other team?" asked Florence absently.

"Paulo must have figured we had less brain power."

"It means it's more difficult for us to move quickly," added Teodoro.

"Are you joining us?" asked Ruby.

He shook his head as he lit another cigarette. "The Princess has asked me to stay here with her."

"I want to be alone," intoned the Princess.

Gayatri shrugged. "Let her be. We'll win soon enough. Besides, we have the ace up our sleeve."

"What ace up our sleeve?" asked Elke.

"Not what, but who. Ruby," said Gayatri.

Ruby smoothed her hair and skirt. "That's generous of you, but I am just another team member. I have an idea, however. I believe the answer is a key."

Jeremy crushed his cigarette in an ashtray. "By gum, she's got it! We'd all be standing in the streets without our house keys."

"But which key? The hotel must have hundreds," said Elke.

The Princess's eyes lit up, like those of a cat hunting a mouse. "It cannot be our room keys. It would be too involved. And the concierge desk is private. The words 'force' and 'strength' imply something difficult to get into."

"A safe?" asked Gayatri.

Elke leaned over the table. "Where are there safes in the hotel?"

"Let's split into pairs," said Florence. "I choose Gayatri. I suggest Jeremy and Iveta pair up. That leaves Ruby and Elke."

Iveta glided forward towards Florence until the two nearly touched noses. "Who made you queen of our team?"

Florence stepped back. "As the Princess's companion, I am acting team queen, or princess, if you will."

Gayatri giggled. "No time for quarrelling. Let's do as Florence suggested."

The group split up and headed in different directions. Ruby and Elke stepped into the concierge area.

"Did you purchase any of the clothes you tried on today?" asked Ruby. "They were divine."

Elke smiled. "I did. A beautiful silk suit. It's perfect for my next trip."

"You won't return home after what has happened?"

Elke traced a finger along her clavicle. "Ah, yes – well, after that. I'm planning a trip to America."

"Is that why you have an American passport?" Ruby looked straight ahead at the concierge desk.

"Oh, no. Yes. I mean – let's ask for the keys." Elke turned to the concierge. "Do you have keys to the safe?"

The young man's eyebrows shot up. "*Por favor*? Perhaps I do not understand."

As Elke cajoled the concierge, Ruby scanned the room. A pair of bookshelves with reading material for the guests stood in a cosy reading nook area. An enormous magenta-coloured grandfather clock stood next to the nook, ticking away pleasantly. Her eyes fixed on the clock. A keyhole!

Leaving Elke behind, Ruby groped around the clock's ledges. The lowest ledge produced nothing but dusty fingers. The second ledge proved fruitful – a small brass key bounced onto the floor.

Click. The narrow door creaked open.

A folded slip of paper sat just behind the pendulum. She reached for it, but just as her fingertips brushed the paper, a gleam caught her eye from the back of the cabinet. Twisting her forearm, she reached further back, patting the wooden base of the cabinet. Her hand landed on a pebble – nothing else. She swept it out of the clock-case, and then her eyes widened.

This was no pebble. A small but perfect diamond sparkled in the palm of her hand.

Looking from side to side, Ruby slipped the jewel into her pocket. Then she took the slip, straightened up, and declared, "I've found the clue, Elke! No need to haggle with the concierge."

30

As the imposter's smile turned into a genuine grin, Fina's worries melted away. Must be her overactive imagination. Now that she felt safe, she cursed Lena's interruption. She was no closer than before to finding out who he really was.

Lena beckoned them again. "Come! I have already read it to the others."

Fina and Salvador fell into step with Lena's erratic march towards the dining room. She waved her hands and sang the next clue:

"Ever eating, ever cloying,
Never finding full repast,
All-devouring, all-destroying,
Till it eats the world at last?"

For a few moments, they were silent, pondering, until the peace was broken by a shriek. The trio dashed into the dining room.

"Whatever is the matter?" The note slipped from Lena's fingers.

Pixley spread out his arms. "I have solved the clue."

"You oaf." Fina put a hand over her heart. "You nearly frightened us to death."

He wiped his bald head back and forth with a handkerchief. "Terribly sorry. Carried away and all that."

"Well?" Salvador held out a hand.

Before Pixley could open his mouth, Makeda said, "The answer is a fire!"

"Right. Let's see. The seashore has a few fire-pits."

"The hotel has fireplaces," said Makeda.

"How about a boiler?" asked Salvador.

"Excellent idea," said Pixley. "Let's split up again."

"Where's the good doctor?"

Fina shivered. "Perhaps he had an epiphany and went in search of the clue. Seems like something he would do."

Makeda mirrored Fina's shiver. "I doubt he'd go off into the night. He might try the fireplaces. I'll show you where they are ... if someone else comes with me."

Fina detected definite fear in Makeda's voice.

"Fina and I will find the boiler." Pixley grabbed her by the arm and piloted her towards the door.

Out of the corner of her mouth Fina said, "You're squeezing me, Pix. What's the matter?"

He whispered, "I'll tell you in a minute."

As they entered the corridor, he said, "After I told Makeda about seeing a strange figure on the balcony—"

"You ninny. Why would you tell her that?"

"Listen. She said she saw a figure on her own balcony. Flashes of purple and red."

"And? Did she receive any threatening notes?"

"She didn't mention it. She thinks this apparition stole her necklace. But she didn't tell her mother because she knew she'd make a scene. I must tell Ruby."

"But I had the sense right now Makeda was afraid of something or someone – not her mother. Why is that?"

"She must have an overactive imagination. Like you."

"Hilarious, Mr Hayford," Fina said as they descended the stairs.

They crept towards the door marked 'boiler' in English and, presumably, Portuguese. A light hum and a gust of warm air came from underneath the door.

Pixley turned the knob and leaned against the door. "It's a trick to stop the door from creaking," he whispered in explanation.

Fina sighed with relief as the door opened. She spied Fausto's back. As if he sensed their presence, he turned around.

"I've got it!" he said, holding up a slip of paper. "I've got it!"

A rumbling, thundering noise came from above them.

Pixley stared at the ceiling. "Sounds like a herd of elephants."

"Last one behind will be bald as an egg!" said Fausto with childish glee. He rushed past them towards the stairs. Pixley ran after him.

"Ow!" Fina twisted her ankle in the rush towards the stairs. She fell against the wall and slid down, feeling sorry for herself. Her stomach growled. Too overwhelmed to do much of anything, she buried her head in her arms. Maybe a moment to herself would give her the strength to face the hordes upstairs.

The light went out.

Gasping, Fina propelled herself upwards by pushing her feet against the floor.

A soft glow filtered down from the stairway, backlighting an approaching figure.

Frozen in place, she watched helplessly as the figure padded towards her.

Her heart, which was previously skipping and sputtering,

suddenly roared to life. Blood pumped through her limbs, causing them to move without her direction. Soon, she was moving backwards in tandem with the approaching figure.

She turned and broke into a mad dash down the corridor.

Half-running, half-hobbling on her twisted ankle, Fina rushed to the boiler room. If she could slip inside and lock the door, she would be safe.

The footsteps behind her were unhurried but deliberate.

She reached the boiler room door. Though it was sticky, she finally forced it open. The hum and warmth of the room enveloped her like her grandfather's hug.

Footsteps approached. She slammed the door, slid the barrel lock into place, and leaned against the door.

The knob jiggled. And jiggled again.

Silence.

The footsteps faded.

She breathed in the damp mildew air. Like freshly tilled earth.

Mind racing, her thoughts jumped from one problem to another. When should she open the door? Where were her friends? Surely they must have missed her by now.

The footsteps returned.

A floorboard creaked behind her. Or was it a door?

She spun round. A figure moved towards her from behind the boiler. Blast it. There was another door to the room!

"Fina?"

"Selkies and kelpies, Idris. You gave me a fright!"

He moved towards her, arms outstretched and a look of shame on his face. "I'll never forgive myself. I thought I had cornered the murderer."

"Murderer? You mean you've been watching us the whole time?"

He moved closer, circling his arms around her. "Yes, I'm

afraid the treasure hunt was my idea. I had second thoughts about it, but once I had mentioned it to Paulo, he refused to give up the scheme. I had the idea it would make something happen."

"But I mistook you for the murderer!"

She gazed into his dark brown eyes and sighed.

He looked around the room. "Rather pleasant in here, isn't it? And private."

"That it is, dear Idris." She moved closer to him.

The boiler hummed gently.

A slow, blood-curdling scream came from the hallway.

31

———

"We have a winner!" Paulo took a glass of champagne from its spot next to a mound of juicy-looking grapes, and lifted it to the Angel's Double Chin team.

Iveta put her arms around Ruby. "And dear Ruby solved it!"

"And me," added Elke. "I solved it with her."

Everyone raised their glasses. Just as they were about to drink, a gust of wind hit the French windows, causing one to open and bounce off the wall. They all turned around with a gasp, and a few champagne flutes wobbled as their owners jumped.

"*Um minutinho!*" Paulo dashed over to secure the door, while the guests peered outside at the palm trees whipping in the gale. As if he were explaining a minor disturbance within his control, Paulo said, "Please excuse the wind, ladies and gentlemen. I believe the storm has finally arrived. Fortunately for us, we need not leave the hotel to celebrate the new year!"

"What is the grape ceremony?" asked Gayatri. "We celebrate the new year at a different time at home. I love learning about different ways to bring in the new."

Pixley whispered to Ruby, "Have you seen Fina?"

Ruby shook her head. "I thought she was with you."

Back at the table, Paulo saluted the winning team. "And now, dear Ruby and Elke, you will be the first ones to experience the famous Muscat grapes! It's one minute until midnight, so you will have the honour of being the first to eat the grapes. One at a time. One for each month of a year, in order to assure happiness in the new year."

"What about everyone else?" asked Ruby.

"They too will have grapes, but the winners must be the first." Paulo offered the two women a bunch of plump red grapes.

Ruby wrinkled her nose. "I'd rather let Elke have them. I'm off grapes at the moment. She deserves recognition."

Shrugging in her characteristic manner, Elke plucked the grapes from Paulo. She plucked one and popped it into her mouth, chewing with exaggerated motion.

The clock chimed one. Two.

Elke selected another. This time she tossed it up and caught it in her mouth like a trained seal.

Everyone clapped. "Bravo!" Iveta moved closer to Elke.

The clock chimed three. Four.

This time, the airborne grape bounced off Elke's face and onto the floor.

And then Elke fell to the floor in convulsions.

"I'm choking!"

Iveta pounced on Elke, lifting her torso upright. Then she slapped her on the back.

Elke continued to choke.

"Someone get a doctor!" yelled Jeremy.

Teodoro dashed out of the room.

A crowd had formed around Elke and Iveta.

Makeda pushed everyone away. "Move, everyone, move. She needs air!"

And then Iveta screamed. Screamed like Tosca throwing herself over the castle walls to her death.

32

Holding hands, Fina and Idris dashed up the stairs.

When they reached the dining room, Idris leapt back into the shadows. Fina nodded at him and continued on.

Shaking at the sight unfolding before her eyes, Fina groped her way towards a seat.

As Iveta let out another scream, Makeda grabbed her mother and held her close.

It was the same scene as last night. Everyone stood around Elke, like figures in a Last Supper painting. Salvador and Ruby paced around one another. Lena cooed over her dog. Fausto's hand propped up his head, as if he shouldered the weight of the world. Florence stood behind the Princess, gripping the chair with all her might. The Princess herself sat with her mouth open. It was the first human reaction Fina had witnessed on the Princess's face. Paulo stood over Elke, shaking his head.

Paulo nodded and clapped his hands. "Ladies and gentlemen. The police will arrive shortly. Please stay where you are. I've asked Mr Rapozo to watch the room while I prepare for Comissário Cardoso."

Fina groaned. Not the elegant detective again.

Gayatri, Pixley, and Ruby looked up at Fina. They rushed over to her as she stood on wobbly legs like a new-born foal.

"We were worried about you. What's the matter?" Ruby asked as she gave Fina an uncharacteristically strong embrace.

"Oh, I ..." Fina waved her hand. "It doesn't matter. Not after what's happened."

Gayatri bit her lip and lowered herself absently into Fina's chair. "It's only dawned on me now. Do you realise what this means?"

Removing his spectacles, Pixley peered closely at Gayatri as if his glasses were an impediment to sight. "What do you mean? Elke is dead."

Her plait flew back and forth as she shook her head vehemently.

Ruby interjected. "Gayatri means the grapes were obviously meant for me. The only people who knew I didn't eat grapes – since our case in Sardinia put me right off all grapes – were the three of you."

"But how could the murderer be certain Ruby would win? And then eat the grapes?" asked Pixley.

Ruby tapped her teeth. "Excellent question."

"If these people are smugglers," said Fina, sweeping one arm around the room with a flourish, "it's plausible they know Ruby is as sharp as a needle. Any one of them might have assumed you'd win the treasure hunt."

"The two skills are entirely unrelated." Gayatri shook her head. "Yes, Ruby is absolutely brilliant – there's little doubt about that – but word puzzles are a particular skill unrelated to detection."

Ruby nodded. "I agree. I'm completely rubbish at word games. It was pure luck I had a go at this one."

"Perhaps the murderer didn't care who died. They just purposely didn't win," said Fina.

Three heads looked at her in disbelief. Then Ruby's frown smoothed out into a smile. "You have a point. The only thing the murderer could be sure of was that he or she would not be the one to eat the grapes."

"And what about Elke?" asked Fina.

"Perhaps the murderer saw an opportunity when we won. They might have just as well tried to poison something else, but saw the grapes as an opportunity."

"But who was the target? You or Elke?" asked Gayatri.

"I'm not sure. It could have been both of us. Hendrik's murderer might think either of us had dangerous knowledge about the case."

Fina surveyed the room.

Cold air streamed in from the corridor.

The police had arrived. Comissário Cardoso led the way, this time dressed in a grey wool suit, with a white cravat. He looked more like a hotel guest than a detective. Fina supposed it might be the reason he had been assigned the case. To put them all at ease.

But the guests were not at ease. They all stared, rooted to the spot, while police flowed like little eddies around them towards the body of Elke Vogel. The police worked quickly, exchanging only brief, grim words from time to time. One took notes on a small notepad.

Makeda, the only one who seemed at all stimulated by the scene, marched up to Cardoso. "What killed her?"

The left side of Cardoso's mouth twitched and spread into a wry smile. "It's not confirmed, but I suppose there's no harm in telling you all. We're pretty certain it was the same thing that killed her husband. Cyanide."

Though Fina expected a collective gasp at the news, none was forthcoming. Did they all know it was cyanide?

Moving away from her position behind the Princess,

Florence stepped haltingly towards Cardoso and Makeda. When she reached them, she turned and faced the audience.

A red lacquered fingernail outstretched towards the crowd. Florence flung her head back and lowered her eyelids.

"You! You killed Elke. For the diamond."

Her finger pointed straight at Miss Ruby Dove.

33

Ruby gulped but remained still as she stared Florence down.

Pixley moved in front of Ruby, as if he were shielding her from a bullet. "I demand an explanation for this outrage." Fina was sure he would add that they should meet at dawn with two pistols.

Florence smirked. Despite her halting step towards Cardoso a minute before, she was now bursting with confidence.

"I saw you." She narrowed her eyes at Ruby's head – the only part of her visible behind Pixley's solid figure. "I spied you taking the jewel from the grandfather clock. When Elke had her back to you at the concierge desk."

Cardoso lifted his hat and ran his fingers through his dark hair. "Is this true, Miss Dove?"

Ruby shook her head. "She's lying. I was at the grandfather clock. But all it contained was the next clue. No diamond." Then she turned out the pockets from her frock and dumped her handbag onto the table. A nearby officer ran his hands over the contents on the table and shook his head.

"She must have hidden it for safekeeping," said Florence, clearly undeterred. "Besides, she was supposed to eat the grapes, not Elke. It means she's the murderer. Only she could have known the grapes were poisoned. Otherwise, she would be dead."

Cardoso looked expectantly at Ruby.

"It's true I don't enjoy grapes—"

"Who doesn't enjoy grapes? I've never heard anything so ridiculous," said Florence.

Fausto stepped forward. "Miss Armitage, I don't see why Miss Dove is the murderer because she didn't eat the grapes. The fact is, the murderer probably wanted to kill Miss Dove, not Mrs Vogel."

Florence held up another red lacquered nail. "But it's not just that. Miss Dove hovered over the grapes as we all entered the dining room after the treasure hunt."

"Treasure hunt?" Cardoso's eyebrows shot up.

"Yes. I'm sure Paulo can explain it to you," said Florence. "What matters is that I saw her spending an inordinate amount of time near the grapes."

"Miss Dove?"

Ruby smoothed her hair. "It's true I did spend time near the grapes. But it's not because I was coating them in poison. It was due to an unfortunate association I have with grapes. I was seeing if that association had vanished. But it hadn't, obviously, otherwise I would have eaten the grapes."

"Utter rot. Balderdash," said Florence. "What a pathetic excuse."

Teodoro had returned and now slipped his arm through Florence's. The gesture was difficult to interpret – was it one of warning, calming, or understanding?

"Hear, hear, as you British say." Lena thumped an empty tumbler on the table. "I knew there was something underhanded about Miss Dove." She threw her head back, mirroring Florence's upturned nose gesture.

Iveta stepped in front of Pixley, now forming a shield of protection two persons deep. "You have no evidence. Pure supposition. Anyone could have tampered with the grapes while Paulo was so manfully securing those doors over there. And how do we know one of you didn't do it?" She pointed at the two women.

"Ladies!" Jeremy intoned in his best stage voice. He stepped forward.

The three women's heads whipped towards him. Gayatri leaned over and whispered to Fina, "If looks could kill ... yet again."

Jeremy stepped backward. A ghost of a smile played across Cardoso's face.

Fina moved towards the centre of the standoff with Gayatri. Gayatri stood tall, all five feet of her, giving Fina a run for her money. "Comissário Cardoso. We are not in court. And these outrageous accusations. We know these people—"

Ruby cut in. "These people are under strain. It's causing us all to snap and say things we'll regret later."

Cardoso nodded. "Wise words, Miss Dove." He turned to Florence. "Have you any actual evidence for the accusation you've made against Miss Dove?"

Florence opened her mouth but Lena held up a finger, as if she were calling for a waiter. "I can, how do you say, collaborate – no, corroborate – Miss Armitage's story. Miss Dove leaned over the grapes for at least two minutes."

A grim line set in across Cardoso's face. He lifted his chin at two nearby officers. "I'm sorry, Miss Dove, but we will need to take you to police headquarters for further questioning."

Pixley remained in front of Ruby. "This is ludicrous. I'm not moving."

"Then we will have to move you, Mr Hayford. Please step aside." Cardoso buttoned his jacket.

Two officers moved stealthily towards Pixley, who held up his hands. "No need. I will come."

"We don't need you to come with us, Mr Hayford. We're only interested in Miss Dove."

Pixley licked his lips. "That's where you're wrong. I killed Elke Vogel."

34

Fina slipped into the corridor. After looking both ways, she tiptoed towards the last doorway.

Tap, tap. Fina winced at the noise she made, however soft it might be.

"Who is it?"

"Fina. I can't sleep. Can you let me in?"

Locks jangled for a few seconds before the door opened. Gayatri rubbed her eyes. "Come in, come in. I couldn't really sleep, either. I tossed and turned."

"May I have a cuppa?" asked Fina as she settled into a red plush chair.

"Yes, I'll put the kettle on. These electric kettles are miraculous, aren't they?"

"I'll say. Been a lifesaver in college."

They stared at one another in silence, listening to the water rumble as it came to a boil.

"What shall we do? How will we rescue Ruby and Pixley? I don't even know if the police have held them for questioning, or if they're in jail."

The water boiled. Though she was clearly half asleep,

Gayatri moved rapidly through tea-making motions. "We must identify the murderer, the ringleader, and who has been watching us."

"Jewels. Emeralds ... a diamond. Ruby."

Gayatri looked up at Fina, as if she were slightly daft. "Yes. Those are jewels ... and our friend is named after one."

Tapping a finger against the bridge of her nose, Fina repeated, "Emerald. Ruby. Diamond. Ruby."

"Are you willing them into existence?" Gayatri frowned and looked at her wristwatch. "It's rather late – or early, I should say. It's gone five o'clock. Perhaps we ought to return to bed."

The darkness outside had turned into the grey filtered light of dawn.

"That's it. That's it!" Fina snapped her fingers. She leapt up, sending her empty teacup and saucer rattling to the floor. "Sorry. Must dash! Please come with me."

Their bare feet slapped against the hardwood floors of the corridor – a great pounding, sticky noise. Gayatri held a finger to her lips and they slowed to a fast tiptoe.

Fina's door was ajar. She could have sworn she'd locked it.

She pressed her fingers lightly against the wood and the door swung open.

A hooded figure stood near the bed, rifling through the bedside table's drawers. Purple and red. Without looking towards Fina and Gayatri, the purple-and-red apparition flew to the open balcony. The billowing, colourful silk spectre vanished into the pinkish dawn.

Hands covering her face, Fina slid down onto the floor, gasping for air.

"Shhh..." said Gayatri, "you've had a shock. I've had a shock. And I've almost convinced myself it was a dream." She gathered a wrap from a nearby chair and draped it over Fina.

Through chattering teeth, Fina said, "Tha-a-a-n-n-k y-o-o-u-u."

"Come on, let's get you into bed." Gayatri pulled Fina to her feet and held her as they lumbered towards the bed. Fina held out a pointing finger.

"Ah, yes. The balcony. Don't worry – I'll shut it. The wraith would've stayed if they had wanted to harm us. They won't be back." She paused. "At least, not for the moment."

The doors to the balcony banged shut. As if a switch had been flicked, Fina stopped shivering and chattering. "I've realised what's happened," she said, and patted the bed next to her. "Sit down and I'll tell you what I know."

Gayatri sat on the bed and crossed her legs under her. "Don't tell me. You know the identity of the apparition."

Fina nodded. "I do. I wish Ruby could witness my deductions, but I'll tell her as soon as we rescue them from the police."

Eyes widening, Gayatri said, "You mean you know who the murderer is as well?"

"I think so. Let me begin with our purple-and-red friend. I've told you about the adventures Pixley, Ruby, and I have had since we last saw you in the summer at Quenby."

"Yes, and while they are legion, I don't remember any purple-and-red murderers among them."

"Have you ever read any Sherlock Holmes stories?"

Gayatri nodded but looked puzzled.

"Remember that devilishly devious cove – Moriarty?"

Though Gayatri's lips parted to make a sound, all that emerged was a croak. Recovering, she said, "Go on."

Twisting the bedclothes around her fingers, Fina continued. "There is this person – possibly a woman, but given what I've heard about the disguises, I really haven't a clue how she identifies herself in reality. But it's neither here nor there. The point is, she has a reason to hate Ruby. And I don't mean dislike intensely. I mean hate. Killing Ruby is not enough for her. And I'm part of it as well."

She faltered. Gayatri patted Fina's hand. "You can tell me the entire backstory later, when we both feel better. Right now, all I need to know is that you believe this Moriarty character – quite apt, given Ruby's deduction skills – is after you and Ruby."

Fina nodded. "It would explain the threatening note with the knife in the melon."

"But why did you suddenly rush to your room?"

Throwing off the bedclothes, Fina slid onto the floor and ran over to the wardrobe. Head half in and half out of the rack of clothes, she said, "Because I remembered the way Ruby gave me a big hug. It seemed extravagant at the time." She emerged triumphant, fist clenched.

"What is it?"

A diamond sparkled in Fina's hand.

Gasping, Gayatri slid off the bed and snatched the gemstone. She held it up to the mauve dawn light. "It's beautiful!"

"That's what our Moriarty friend was looking for. You see, Ruby slipped the diamond into my pocket when she gave me a hug."

"But why? And why would she have it?"

"She knew that out of the four of us, I would be the least likely to be searched, given my light skin and the status it brings. As for why she had it, all I can surmise is that she found it, as Florence said, on the treasure hunt."

Plait flying back and forth, Gayatri shook her head. "Why wouldn't Ruby admit it, and why would she try to hide it? It doesn't make any sense."

"I have a feeling she knows who the murderer is. Or suspects. And I also think she realised Moriarty is on our trail."

"You mean this is so dangerous she wanted to protect us by going to the jail?"

"More than that, I think she needed to protect herself by doing so."

35

———

"That blasted clock won't stop ticking. Can't someone make it stop?" Pixley paced in front of the bench where Ruby lay, shielding her eyes with her arm from the overhead light.

"Mmmmm…" was all she replied.

He bent over her. "Are you asleep?"

"I drifted. But I'm not anymore." She did not remove her arm.

"What shall we do?"

"We're safe here. I am a little worried about Fina and Gayatri, though."

"Will you look at me?" Pixley pushed his spectacles further up his nose, as if they would help him see through Ruby's arm and into her eyes.

She moved her arm back into its usual position at her side. "Sorry. The light is horrid."

He looked up in acknowledgement at the buzzing institutional fixture. "Well, we are in a police station. I don't expect it to be cosy."

Ruby scowled and slid her arm back over her eyes.

"My apologies!" Pixley's hands waved about wildly. "We're in a tight spot, but we've been in plenty before. You could say the others were worse."

Ruby's arm moved just enough so one eye blinked at him sceptically.

"What I mean is, I know I haven't committed the crime, and you know you haven't committed a crime."

Her body shot up. "Pix, I realise we're tired, but what are you babbling on about? When have we ever committed murder?"

Pixley lowered himself onto a rickety bench opposite Ruby. "I mean it's not as bleak as it seems." He paused. "What did you mean when you said, 'We're safe here'? I don't consider the jail to be safe."

Ruby gave Pixley one of her smiles that was a mixture of genuine warmth and the condescension of a kindly nanny. "I see. You think I gave in once Florence accused me. I know you piped up out of loyalty – but you think the police have something on me, don't you?"

Pixley frowned. "Well, don't they?"

She shook her head. "Someone slipped a note in my pocket during the treasure hunt. It read, 'Give in. From I.'"

"That's it? *Give in.* And from that you deduced you should allow yourself to be arrested?"

"We've not technically been arrested, though. We're being held for questioning."

Pixley looked around the dingy cell, eyes fixing momentarily on the faint light streaming in through the barred window. "Seems it's one and the same." He waved his hand dismissively. "Go on, please."

"I didn't know what it meant at the time. But I assumed the 'I' must mean it was from Idris. When Florence accused me, I figured that was the moment I should give in."

"But to what end? I don't understand. Why does Idris want us to end up in a police station, of all places?"

Ruby smoothed her hair and skirt. "The purple-and-red figure. That's why. You realise who it is, don't you?"

Leaning forward, Pixley pulled up one trouser leg. "I wish you'd tell me."

"It's our friend from Marsden Court."

"No. It can't be. You mean it's–"

A hand shot up, halting Pixley in his tracks. "Don't invoke the name. Please. I'm not superstitious, but I made Fina promise she'd never say the name again. It will give this person more power over us."

"So how shall I refer to her?"

"How about 'Professor'?"

"Why on earth would you call our nemesis a professor?"

Ruby gave a little sigh. "Don't you enjoy detective stories?"

"Frankly, with our escapades, I scarcely have time to read anything, regardless of whether it's detective fiction or the newspaper."

She chuckled. "It's true, isn't it? No, I meant Professor Moriarty. In Sherlock Holmes. It has an elegant ring to it since Fina and I are only students in college."

"Professor it is, then. Now we've sorted the nomenclature, will you tell me what is going on?"

"The Professor has been following us – she's the figure in purple and red. She's also the person who put the threatening note next to Fina's bed."

"So the Professor is the murderer?"

Ruby shook her head. "Far from it. But I believe the Professor *is* part of this smuggling ring. Perhaps tangentially."

"The Professor couldn't have followed us all the way from England simply to threaten us."

Ruby rubbed her eyes. "It's clear she wants something from us. Revenge? I'm not sure what it is. But I don't think she wants to kill us. She's had plenty of opportunities to do that."

"But you know who the murderer is?"

Without saying anything, Ruby nodded, with closed eyes.

"Miss Ruby Dove, you can be the most exasperating person at times." Pixley jiggled his leg.

Her eyelids flew up like a shudder. "I'm sorry, Pix, but it's—"

"For my own good." He adjusted his spectacles. "So, what shall we do now? Why don't you tell the police who it is so we can bring this wretched affair to a close?"

"I cannot tell them. Yet. Because I'm certain the Professor is at the hotel. And Fina and Gayatri are in danger."

"So what's your suggestion?"

"We need to ensure the Professor will not interfere when we speak to the suspects. I'm almost certain who the murderer is, but I need to clear up a few loose ends before I'm sure."

Pixley grinned. "I have an idea."

36

The wheels screeched and squeaked.

A merry little bell chimed.

Fina held on to the armrest as they lurched around the corner. She was glad she hadn't eaten that second pastry at breakfast.

The driver of the yellow tram grunted as a young man flew across the street, leaving scattered pigeons in his wake.

Lena's peppery perfume had settled into the general atmospheric soup of the tram. Fina wrinkled her nose, hoping the driver would open the door for a minute to let the smell of the bakery nearby replace that of the oppressive perfume.

Gayatri leaned over and whispered, "I'm terribly confused. Why are we all on a tram? It was on my list of tourist activities to do in Lisbon, but I scarcely expected it to be a police-escorted tram."

Admiring the children hopping about like robins in a nearby schoolyard, Fina shook her head. "I'm as much in the dark as you are. When Cardoso told us we were going to Lisbon, I thought it would be to visit Ruby and Pixley. I had no idea everyone else from the hotel would be here – much less on a tram!"

The tram screeched and halted. The occupants all slid forward on the benches lining the inside of the carriage.

Cardoso thumped to the front of the carriage and nodded at the driver. Across the street, Fina saw Pixley nimbly tiptoeing in between cars, followed by a figure in a navy frock and a cream Florentine floppy hat. Ruby!

Cardoso waved Pixley and Ruby aboard the tram. The door snapped shut immediately following their entrance. Still standing in the entryway, Cardoso turned towards the crowd. The tram jerked and then made its way up a small incline.

"Ladies and gentlemen." Cardoso removed his elegant hat and held it against his chest. "I realise this is highly irregular, but Miss Dove and Mr Hayford have convinced me it is the best – or rather the only – way to capture the murderer of Mr and Mrs Vogel."

"This is outrageous. Who solves murders on a moving tram?" Fausto rose a little out of his seat. Then he plopped back down and wiped his forehead with a handkerchief. *Well, well,* thought Fina. It was the first time she had seen the good Doutor act shaken. Perhaps Cardoso's scheme was a good idea.

Grasping the pole with one gloved hand and her hat with another, Ruby began her tale. "Thank you all for your patience. Believe me when I say this arrangement is for our safety. Possibly even the safety of the murderer."

Cici yapped. Lena smoothed down his ears. "You've upset Cici."

"On the contrary, Miss Fieraru." Pixley reached into his pocket and pitched a bit of dried meat onto the floor. "He's quite enjoying himself."

Ruby cleared her throat. Pixley took his seat next to Gayatri.

"We have had two murders that remained unsolved. There are a few loose ends to tie up before we reveal the murderer."

Florence gave an uncharacteristic snort from behind her little red lacquer hat.

"Let's begin with the victims. What do we know about the Vogels?"

Gayatri raised a hand eagerly. "They were chocolate importer-exporters."

"Correct."

"Next you'll give us top marks for our maths papers." Jeremy sat sulkily in the corner of the carriage, arms crossed. He peered out of the window, as if he couldn't be bothered with these trite proceedings. But his unshaven face and puffy eyelids told a different story.

Cardoso waved his hat at Jeremy. "Please, Mr Salter. No more interruptions, or I shall be forced to take more serious measures." Fina detected a slight grin of sadistic pleasure on the Comissário's face.

"Thank you, Comissário." Ruby leaned against a pole near the entrance. "The Vogels were importer-exporters. Which means they were likely central to the smuggling ring."

"What smuggling ring?" Makeda's eyes grew wide.

"A smuggling ring designed to serve the wealthy and famous. Its purpose is to maintain people's positions in power. Funds are needed usually to suppress rebellions by various workers and local populations subject to the whims of colonial landowners. And potentially to pay off or persuade European officials to look the other way. A particularly brutal example happened to chocolate farmers in Guinea-Bissau – Pixley told me about the atrocities that were never publicised. We're afraid another similar, larger-scale situation is brewing in Sierra Leone. And for those involved in the ring who aren't powerful themselves, they could make a tidy profit ensuring those powerful people remain so."

"Gordon Bennett!" muttered Jeremy under his breath. "Who in God's name have I been taking up?"

"I knew it!" cried the man calling himself Salvador. He jumped up. "They all want to maintain the evil colonial system. To profit from tea, gems and chocolate."

Ruby's left eyebrow raised, ever so slightly. "Quite correct about the purpose of the ring. And about what is being smuggled. How do you know so much about it, Mr, er, Carvalho?"

After a strangled sound arose from his throat, Salvador regained control. "Because of who I am. You all know how I feel about Portuguese control of Goa. It isn't a secret."

"But why are you staying at a resort like Estoril? How does it advance your cause?" asked Florence.

He ran his finger up and down through his moustache. "For the reason Miss Dove has outlined already. I wanted to know more about this smuggling ring, which I'm quite certain helps maintain Salazar's power."

"Hear, hear." Fausto stamped his foot. "That's why I'm here."

Pixley leaned forward. "Is it, Doutor Tavares? I believe I've seen you with some jewellers' receipts."

"Why yes, of course. I came to meet Salvador here. He wrote to me some months ago. We have mutual interests – he, like myself, believes in the cause of fighting for the oppressed peoples of the world, the downtrodden, those who cannot fight for themselves – and through our correspondence, we hatched a plan. I am an honourable man, Miss Dove, and so I will lay it all before you. We planned to skim smuggling ring proceeds to fund our own cause. To overthrow the Portuguese from running Cape Verde, once and for all. Those receipts were just cover for the emeralds in case there were any police questions."

"Fausto!" Iveta's scarlet silk sleeves fluttered and flapped. Cici yapped and ran underneath the bench.

"It's true, darling. I'm here to see you, of course, but also for another reason."

Iveta put her hands on her hips and heaved a great sigh.

Ruby looked at Paulo. "Do you want to tell Iveta or shall I?"

Paulo's ever-present grin vanished. He leaned back, put his arm across the seat and tapped his fingers in a defiant gesture of nonchalance. Except his fingers shook. "I don't know what you're talking about."

"The good Doutor is a mathematician. He had some papers with equations in his room. But not just any equations—"

Fausto stamped his foot, rose to his full height and nearly bumped his head on the metal rail. "How dare you! You were in my room! My private papers."

Iveta scrunched up her face. "Be quiet, Fausto. I want to hear what dear Ruby has to say." She smiled sweetly at Ruby.

"You were being paid by the casino to help them with some mathematical problems, weren't you?"

"Rubbish." Fausto sat back down and crossed his arms. Then he kicked the pole in front of him.

Pixley pointed at Paulo. "I saw the documents myself. How can you deny it?"

Paulo shrugged. "I don't deny it. But you don't understand how casinos run. We have to make sure we won't lose all of our money. We sometimes hire experts to make sure that doesn't happen."

Teodoro's toothpick danced up and down at the corner of his mouth. "You mean the entire time I've been working at the casino, I didn't know the games were rigged? Which games were rigged?"

Paulo wagged a finger at Teodoro and chuckled. "Ah! You are a good actor, Teo. You knew all about it."

In a flash, Teodoro leapt across the carriage and shook Paulo. "You idiot. How dare you say I'm a liar."

"*Silêncio, por favor!*" The Comissário stepped forward and put a warning hand on Teodoro's shoulder. "While I appreciate the information about the casino, Miss Dove, it is immaterial to the crime. What's more, I'm afraid there are few laws regulating this type of gambling, so while the practice may be ethically questionable, it isn't illegal."

Spreading his hands out towards Teodoro, Paulo said, "Nothing to be worried about, Teo."

Lena thumped her foot. "But let us return to the good doctor and Mr Carvalho. I knew there was something suspicious about the two of them."

Ruby smoothed her skirt and moved back into her position, even as the tram made a sharp turn. "Doutor Tavares and this man here both wanted to use the ring for two purposes. The first was to infiltrate it for information that might be beneficial to their respective causes in Goa and Cape Verde. Second, they wanted to divert any of the goods they could get their hands on for themselves."

"Which is why they exchanged an emerald at the monastery," said Gayatri.

Fina scanned the car to see if anyone had reacted to this news. But they were all too practised at keeping that particular emotion of surprise at bay.

"Precisely."

"But why was Teodoro at the monastery as well?" asked Lena. "Was he also part of this small counter-ring within the smuggling ring?"

Fina had discussed with Gayatri what would happen if Teodoro's secret about watching the Princess were revealed. He would likely be executed, along with any of his confederates.

Fina wondered if Ruby had come to the same conclusion, especially as they hadn't had time to tell her what they thought.

Ruby's eyes flickered. "I expect Teodoro was watching Salvador and Fausto on behalf of the Princess. Isn't that correct, Teodoro?"

The toothpick dropped from his mouth and rolled the length of the carriage until Cici chased after it and began to chew on it.

"Ah. Yes. You're correct, Miss Dove." His tense shoulders drooped. "I thought something was odd about those two, so I decided to follow them."

Pixley looked about to burst.

Gayatri shook her head very gently. Pixley grimaced but nodded in reply.

The Princess took Teodoro's hand. "Darling Teo, where would I be without you?"

Ruby quickly redirected the discussion after looking at Pixley's face. "But the most important point about all of this was not the emerald." She nodded at Gayatri.

Gayatri stood up, biting her lip. She pointed at Salvador.

"You're an imposter."

37

———

Salvador ran a finger through his collar. "I'm sorry, Miss Badarur. Did you say imposter?"

Gayatri clapped her hands. "Yes. Now more than ever, I'm sure I'm right. That first night, when I met you outside the hotel, I thought you looked remarkably different to the man I had heard at college. But your manner was so similar, it crossed my mind that I might be mistaken. But then I just remembered—"

"Spectacles," said Ruby.

Salvador's hand shot up to hold on to his owlish spectacles.

Gayatri looked at Ruby in wonder. "Yes, but how did you know?"

"I've been keeping an eye on him, too."

The Comissário sighed. "Please tell us, Miss Dove."

But Gayatri was the one who responded. "When we were in the casino the night Hendrik died, Salvador had left his spectacles on the roulette table. It was later that Teodoro returned them to him. Now, it would be one thing if they were reading glasses, but I remembered he never took them off at Oxford. He should have missed them after a minute or two. But he didn't."

"And therefore he is an imposter!" cried Lena. "I knew it. Treacherous swine."

"Wait a moment," said Jeremy. "Is that the reason I never flew him anywhere? He thought I'd realise he was an imposter? But I never met him before."

"I suspect it was because the real Salvador Carvalho was somewhere else at the time, and this imposter feared you might read about an appearance in the newspaper and realise that a person couldn't be in two places at once," said Ruby.

Jeremy let out a low whistle. "So who are you?"

Head in hands, Salvador said in a muffled voice, "I'm his cousin, Kamath."

Fausto stood up and moved stealthily towards the hunched-over body of Salvador's cousin. "You, you..." A stream of Portuguese invective followed.

"Yes, Fausto. I'm sure Kamath wanted the emeralds for himself. In the process, however, he could have severely hindered your own plans in Cape Verde."

Fausto plopped back down on his seat. His fist unclenched. "At least I know now. And I'm grateful to you for that, Miss Dove. But how is this relevant?"

A murmur of approval and nodding heads ensued.

"I appreciate your patience." Ruby held up a hand. "But we must review everyone's connections to the smuggling ring to understand these murders. Now, let's discuss the other two people you have connections with – Iveta and Makeda."

Iveta put an arm around Makeda's shoulder. "Leave her alone. She's just a child."

Ruby ignored Iveta's plea. "I noticed you and Fausto were easy in each other's company. Like old friends. Or lovers."

"Pah!" exclaimed Iveta. "We are old friends. I first met Fausto on a trip to Cape Verde, no, Faustinho? Must have been 1919."

Fausto coughed. "Ah, yes. It must have been then." His eyes

flickered, as if he were back in 1919. "Remember that little cafe near the water?"

The Comissário's jacket brushed forward past Fina. "Reminiscences are lovely, but can we return to the murder?"

Pixley held up a forefinger. "1919. That's seventeen years ago. How old are you, Makeda?"

"Seventeen," she responded quickly. Her hand covered her mouth. "You don't mean..." She turned to Iveta. "But Mama, you said Papa had died at sea."

Iveta's eyes flashed. As her hand rose, Fausto grabbed it and squeezed. "It's better this way, darling. You planned to tell her anyway."

Iveta cooed, "Makeda, it is difficult, but with time..."

Makeda's wide eyes narrowed. "*Falar pelos cotovelos*. You speak with the elbows – you speak too much! What do you know about it? You have had your hands all over Fausto ever since we arrived."

Fina had a sudden impulse, especially as Ruby seemed to avoid the question. "But Makeda, you're not as innocent as you make out, are you?"

Jeremy murmured, "Quite the little firecracker, aren't you, dear Fina?"

Fina squashed the desire to sock Jeremy squarely on the jaw. "I saw you steal a bottle of perfume in the shops in Estoril. And given the ease with which you accomplished that task, I imagine it's not the first time you've stolen something."

Gayatri wriggled in her seat. "And you must have been the one to set off the fire alarm! To give you a chance to steal your own necklace. One that your mother was likely to sell. You knew you could get a better price for it, and keep the money safe."

Pixley let out a low whistle.

Paulo cracked open a window and gulped in the air.

"Please, Mr Mariz, close the window. It is for your own safety."

He did as he was told. But he could not settle into his own seat.

"One moment," said Pixley. "Paulo realised Makeda had set off that alarm, didn't you, Paulo?"

"Ravings. Mere ravings of a delusional scandal-mongering journalist." Paulo threw up his hands.

Fina did not want to be distracted by Paulo's involvement. "Well?" She pointed at Makeda. "Do you deny the theft? Did you set off the alarm?"

"But why would she steal her own necklace?" asked Florence.

Iveta clicked her tongue against her front teeth. "Dearest Makeda has a bit of a habit, shall we say."

"I'm sorry, Miss Da Silva. Iveta, I mean." Pixley pulled up a trouser leg. "That might explain the perfume theft, but not an elaborate charade to steal one's own necklace."

The Comissário nodded. "Tell us, Miss Da Silva. Makeda."

Lifting her head up from her mother's shoulder, Makeda's eyes blazed. "You all think I'm a terrible person, but I am not!" She grabbed the nearest pole and hoisted herself up. "You're all against me!"

38

"What is it, darling?" Iveta took her daughter's oval face into her hands. "Please calm down. It is not time for a scene."

Fina thought this gentle scolding was unfair to Makeda. After all, her mother was one of the most impressive scene-makers she had ever witnessed.

"Mama. I'd better tell them." Makeda removed her mother's hands. "I'm not a thief. Not a compulsive one, at least."

"I knew it." The Princess made the statement as if she were discussing the weather. "That one has the face of a thief. See how her eyes move side to side?"

Makeda ignored the Princess. "My mother loves life – as you all can see. Sometimes her lust to live life to its fullest outpaces her own bank account. I've seen the bank statements. I know we are doomed if she continues to spend. That's why I stole the perfume. To sell it later. The money goes into a separate bank account, a secret one, where she can't touch it."

The Comissário waved his hat. "And the necklace?"

"I planned to steal more than the necklace, but I didn't have time. I knew the gems were insured and we would receive that money. As my mother is in the gem trade, I also know a few people to whom I could sell the jewels I took. Then we would be out of the woods."

Not a muscle on the normally expressive face of Iveta moved. A single tear streamed down her cheek, as if it were raining inside the carriage.

"Dear Iveta." Fausto's lips barely moved. "I assure you all that while Iveta tangled in this smuggling ring, she doesn't understand it's designed to maintain certain interests. She is just a supplier."

As if to confirm this, Iveta's eyebrows furrowed as her eyes bulged. "What do you mean? You mean I've been helping to prop up those scoundrels in power around Europe?"

Gayatri, Pixley, and Fina exchanged glances. Glances of disbelief. Could this woman really be that naive?

Makeda sniffed and rocked her mother's shoulders back and forth. "That's why we love her. Everyone thinks I'm the innocent because of my age."

Fausto puffed up his chest. "You've inherited your father's wisdom."

Fina touched Ruby on the arm, then whispered into her ear, "What about the conversation I overheard between her and Elke? The afternoon before Elke was murdered?"

"Thanks, Feens. I forgot about it."

Ruby straightened up. "Dear Iveta, I fear I must pry into your love affairs a little more. Was Elke your lover?"

Makeda gasped and gave a little nod. She rubbed her mother's back. "I suspected as much. As my mother seems at a loss for words, it's better that I confirm it so you don't think she was the murderer."

"But if they quarrelled – which admittedly seemed minor when I overheard it – wouldn't that give her a motive?" asked Fina.

Iveta pressed her fingers so far into her eye sockets Fina

feared she might go blind. She sighed. "It's true about the affair. But that was all. It was coming to an end as we constantly squabbled. I had no wish to harm her."

The Princess shifted in her seat. "This is quite a touching scene, but may we get on with it? This carriage car is stifling." She held a hand to her forehead. "Would you give me my pills, Florence?"

With one deft motion, Florence withdrew a brown bottle so packed with pills it didn't make a noise.

The Princess tipped out a healthy portion into her gloved hand and inserted them, one by one, into her mouth.

Everyone stared at her.

When she finished her task, the Princess surveyed the crowd and shrugged. "Why are you all staring at me? I take pills for my nerves."

"The doctor prescribed these special pills for the Princess," Florence put in. "They're only available in Romania."

"Did you check the Princess's pills?" Jeremy waved a cigarette at the Comissário.

"For what?" Florence's shoulders stiffened.

"For poison, you ninny," said Jeremy.

The Princess's alabaster-white face drained of what little blood it had. She put a hand to her throat. "You mean the doctor has been poisoning me?"

Fina's mind bobbed and weaved as she tried to recall the details of the past few days. Something about a chemist. Yes.

"Lena Fieraru's father was a chemist. Isn't that true?" Ruby smiled at Lena.

"You English are so very clever, aren't you? Think you know everything." She shrugged and massaged Cici's ears. "Yes, he was a chemist. But that hardly makes me a murderer. I know little about chemistry. Besides, how would I be able to access the Princess's pills? She hates me. As does Miss Armitage."

Pixley banged his hand on the bench. "It's true you did not have access to the pills directly, but we saw you talking to Florence in the garden." He turned to the Princess. "How do you feel after taking the pills?"

The Princess tilted her head to one side. "I'm relaxed. But sometimes a little too relaxed. And I have terrible dreams."

"That's because the pills aren't strong enough," interjected Florence. "I told the doctor he should increase the dosage. That's why you are so often confused."

The Comissário looked at Ruby and nodded.

Ruby turned to the Princess. "Are you saying you think these pills cause confusion and fatigue?"

Clasping her hands together, the Princess replied, "Yes. I feel peculiar after taking them. But every time I mentioned it to Florence, she said it was because I didn't have enough of the pills."

Ruby cleared her throat. "I've suspected for some time that Florence used pills to control you."

Florence snorted. "Utter tosh. Why would I want to do that? I have a perfectly lovely position by her side." She smiled at the Princess.

Fina leapt up. "How can you afford to buy all of those expensive perfumes? Ruby and I saw you buy them in the shop."

"I scrimp and save. My living costs are quite low."

Ruby nodded at Fina. Fina decided to take a different tack. "Why were you talking to Lena in the garden? We saw you chatting away merrily. What on earth would you two have to discuss?"

Florence's eyes darted towards Lena. Lena sniffed.

"You two were in league together. Lena paid you, Florence, to administer mind-altering pills to the Princess, with the goal of eventually killing her. So Lena could become Queen. At least, that's the fantasy she had," said Fina.

Cici leapt out of Lena's arms and shot off like a cannon towards Fina. He growled and sank his teeth into her skirt. Fina bent down, grabbed the offender and opened his jaws. Cici went still, clearly not used to being stopped in his tracks.

Pixley chuckled. "Where'd you learn to do that, Feens?"

"Growing up in the countryside has its advantages."

A stream of Romanian issued forth from Lena. Fina was glad she understood none of it as she marched Cici back to her owner.

Jeremy shot up. "I've got it! Lena and Florence killed Hendrik and Elke Vogel because they discovered something about their plan to kill – or at least control – the Princess!"

"Bravo, Mr Salter," said Ruby with a smile. "But it's not quite true, is it, Princess Thalia?"

"Whatever do you mean, Miss Dove?"

The Comissário bent over so his face was level with the Princess's. "She means that those pills are nothing but soda mints."

39

A great crash and a tinkling of glass echoed inside the carriage.

The tram lurched to a halt and the lights flickered momentarily. And then burned out.

Fina opened the window but before she could pop her head out, Ruby pulled her back and slammed it shut. "Moriarty, Feens. Moriarty."

If it hadn't been for Ruby's support, Fina would have slithered to the floor like a pat of butter slipping off a warm scone.

Cardoso signalled to the driver and dashed outside. A moment later, he returned. "Ladies and gentlemen. Someone left a crate of wine on the tracks." Fina couldn't tell if his sad tone was because of the crash or losing a crate of wine. "We must hurry off this tram. It is for your safety."

Jeremy pointed across the street. "There's a hotel across the street. Why don't we meet in there?"

Cardoso rubbed his chin. "No. I do not think so. Follow me." He pointed at another yellow tram, merrily clanging its bell as pedestrians and carts weaved around it.

Like ducklings trailing behind their mother, the passengers dutifully made their way onto the next tram. Cardoso's flash of a police card saved them from having to fish for change in their pockets.

The locals stared in wonder at their little party, overdressed for a jaunt on the number II tram. Cici wriggled under Lena's tight grasp at the sight of a pail full of freshly caught fish.

At the next stop, Cardoso waved them off the tram and hurried through a green door. Though the front of the building held no sign, Fina spied a group of chairs and a table with a bottle of wine on it.

Eyes adjusting to the gloom, Fina made out a long bar along one wall and a large circular table in the corner. Cardoso murmured a few words to a bald-headed man in an open-necked white shirt. The man slapped Cardoso on the back and piloted him to the large table.

Gayatri whispered, "What are we doing here? Is this a trap?"

As if in answer to her question, a scraping noise of keys turning in the lock came from the front door.

Cardoso pulled out chairs, one by one, for the guests, as if he were *maître d'* in a West End restaurant. Reluctantly, the guests complied. Except Lena.

"When will this charade will be over? And why did you lock us in?"

Ruby glanced at Cardoso, ready to speak. She shut her mouth as Cardoso gently shook his head. "Madam, we've come here for your protection. Even to protect the murderer."

The bald-headed man arrived with a tray of *bicas*. The tiny espresso cups made it look like they were all children, playing at having a tea party.

A murmur of approval circled the table. Ruby seized the moment, stood up and leaned against the back of her chair.

"Now, let us continue."

"Soda mints," said Fausto.

"Correct. Soda mints. This raises a few questions. Could the soda mints have replaced a bottle of cyanide capsules? That doesn't seem very plausible, as one only needed a few capsules and it would be extraordinarily dangerous to keep them in a regular medicine bottle. The other option is that Florence thought the pills were dangerous for the Princess's health, so she replaced them with soda mints."

Florence and the Princess mirrored one another as they sat perfectly still, lips pursed. Only the Princess's ringlets quivered.

Pixley lit a cigarette, waving away the smoke from Fina's face. "That seems implausible. What's the other option?"

"The other possibility is that the Princess came to suspect that her companion – under the guidance of Lena – was trying to control, or perhaps even kill, her. She replaced the pills with the soda mints to fool them. I first had this idea when I noticed how steady the Princess's hand was when we were in the perfume shop," said Ruby.

Teodoro shifted in his seat. "I've seen Lena and Florence chatting. Why else would they speak to one another – at least on polite terms?"

"Traitor," spat out Lena.

"You fool!" cried Florence, suddenly coming alive.

A slow smile spread across the Princess's face. She tapped her fingers lightly on the white tablecloth. "Yes, I knew those two were trying to control me. I don't think they were trying to poison me, because I would have died by now. But yes, the first time I took the prescribed pills – undoubtedly procured by Lena, given her access to a chemist – I had visions and saw things that weren't there. I soon realised what was happening. I had to play along by feigning a kind of feverish illness."

"I can see Lena's motive to control you – and to eventually kill you – but not Miss Armitage's motive," said Pixley.

"I suspect it was simple greed," said Ruby. "After I saw her brooch, I wondered how Miss Armitage could afford such luxuries. Granted, she travelled with a princess, but it still seemed too ostentatious for someone who was a paid companion. Lena was supplying her with funds in exchange for her help."

"Surely Teodoro must have known something about these plans." The Comissário absentmindedly adjusted the hat on his knee.

Ruby was quick to respond, even as Teodoro opened his mouth. "Teodoro knew, of course, about Lena's affair with the King, but he did not know about this little arrangement between Lena and Florence. They went to great lengths to make their relationship appear antagonistic."

"That leaves Mr Mariz and Mr Salter as the only two who we've not discussed in terms of the smuggling ring – besides the four of you." The Comissário winked at Fina.

"Yes, Cardoso, why haven't you picked apart *their* motives?" A cloud of cigarette smoke obscured Jeremy's face.

"They were actually among my first suspects. But I possess reliable information that they were not involved in the smuggling, or with the murders."

"But that's preposterous!" Florence slammed her fist on the table. "I saw Miss Dove near the grapes."

"You may all try as you might to divert us from our purpose, but it will do nothing in the end. Please proceed, Miss Dove."

"Jeremy Salter. His tussle with Mr Mariz that first day was peculiar..."

"I can explain," said Paulo.

"We'll come to you in a moment, Mr Mariz. Now, Jeremy is quite obviously integral to this smuggling ring, as he is a pilot. He flies members of the ring to various places, which allows them to conveniently smuggle gems in particular around the continent."

"I fly whoever pays me a decent rate," said Jeremy nonchalantly. "And that happens to be wealthy people. For example,

Salvador here – Kamath – slipped a note in my pocket the night of the murder that said he wanted me to fly him as far away from Estoril as possible."

Kamath, who had his head between his hands, nodded.

"I keep my mouth shut and don't ask questions, either. And I haven't any control over what they pack in their luggage. I'm not a customs official."

"Then why did you try to kill us in your aeroplane?" Fina asked quietly.

A gasp rippled around the table.

Jeremy leaned forward across the table, waving away the cigarette smoke as if he had not produced it himself.

"Listen, little girl. It was a mechanical malfunction. Haven't you ever heard of those?"

Pixley snorted. "What rot. I've heard the story and it sounds to me as if you were afraid you had been discovered – most likely as the murderer – and you did your best to scare the wits out of Fina and Ruby."

"And me!" cried Lena. "I was certain we were all going to die!"

Jeremy's lips pulled back into a wolf-like smile. "And we certainly were headed towards the pearly gates. Or the gates of hell, as the case may be." He held his grin and turned it on Ruby. "But I saved us all in the end, didn't I?"

He leaned back in his chair. "Besides all that, I suspect our good friend Mr Mariz tampered with the plane."

Paulo licked his lips and withdrew a handkerchief as worn as a cut corn-stalk from his inside pocket. "No, no. This is ludicrous! Why should I do such a thing! Yes, I have interests in Estoril, but that is what a good businessman does."

"Absolutely." Ruby leaned over her chair. "And being the local head of the smuggling ring makes it even more important, doesn't it?"

40

Paulo's pasty-white face turned purple. He wiped his brow.

Cardoso drew a line along his jaw with a forefinger. "No need to deny it, Mariz. We've suspected you for some time. Best come clean, especially if you're not the murderer."

"Murderer!" His handkerchief was sopping wet now. "Oh, no. Yes, yes, yes, I am involved in the smuggling ring. Only locally, you see. Who is the ringleader? I don't know – I just do their bidding. They send me notes and I receive the money. You must trust me."

Pixley gasped. "That's why the hotel room locks were tampered with! Paulo must have rigged them for easy entry and exit."

"Why would he need to do that if he's the manager?" asked Fina.

"Because it's not only him who needs access. Remember, he's just the local ringleader," said Ruby.

Jeremy removed his jacket.

"Looks like you're getting ready for a fight, Mr Salter. Much like that incident in the corridor, remember?"

Fina jumped up. Seeing the stares, she sat back down.

"Jeremy and Paulo had a scuffle. They were wrestling. What got you so worked up, Jeremy?"

He said nothing but glared at Fina.

"Please tell us," said Cardoso.

Silence.

"Let me guess. You wanted out of this racket, but Paulo wasn't keen to let you go. He had a hold over you. Isn't that right?"

Jeremy's cigarette tumbled out of his open mouth. "How did you know?"

"You and Paulo had a confrontation. Then Fina and I overheard Paulo mentioning how difficult you were. And then, when we were flying high above Estoril, you told us how restless you were and that you couldn't stick to anything that long. I surmised that Paulo must have been trying to keep you in place. As the pilot, you were an integral part of the operation."

Cardoso leaned forward. "Is this true, Mr Salter?"

Jeremy's usual suave manner melted away. "I'll admit to it, but only because it should clear me of the murder. That's the only thing I had to hide. Besides, once I'd taken care of Mariz, I planned to clear out of Estoril forever. The first murder made that difficult."

"What information did Paulo have to hold over you?" asked Gayatri.

Paulo said, "He had an affair. With someone who was married. And the partner – let's just say they would not have taken the news well. Violence would have ensued, most likely. That's enough – no need for the details."

"Glad to see you have some principles intact, Mariz," sighed Jeremy.

"Now we've cleared that up, we'll proceed to the Vogels," said Ruby. "It's clear how you all had motives – at least in theory – to kill them if they knew something that would expose you. Even though we cannot prove the Princess, Miss Fieraru, and Miss Armitage were connected to the smuggling ring, they have secrets to hide."

A grey cat loped in from the back of the cafe. This superior animal considered itself to be the primary owner and host.

Cici yapped. Lena squeezed the dog in her arms.

"What is on that cat's tail?" Makeda pointed to something dragging along behind it.

Fina blinked. It was round and sausage-like. And the end of it glowed.

In a flash, Gayatri grabbed a jug of water from the table and poured it over the cat. A fierce howl ensued from the soaked animal.

"*Istenem*, my God!" cried the normally unflappable Teodoro. "Did you see that? It was a stick of dynamite!"

Chairs scraped and fell over as everyone jumped up from the table. The tablecloth caught on Jeremy's chair and slid off, taking the cups and saucers with it. The crash muffled Lena's and Florence's screams.

Amidst the chaos, Fina scanned the room. Gayatri grabbed Pixley's hand, pulling him up from the floor.

Cardoso brushed off splashes of coffee from his suit. Fina touched his shoulder. "Where's Ruby?"

An open-mouthed Cardoso gestured noiselessly, as if pantomiming a fish.

And then, out of the shadows, came two figures, mimicking panthers on the hunt.

Ruby.

And Idris.

~

A FLY BUZZED against the window, hitting it repeatedly, like a drunken sailor.

The door to the police interview room opened and in walked Idris and Cardoso.

Idris winked at Fina, instantly calming her tense muscles while simultaneously stirring up a nest of hornets in her stomach.

Cardoso dragged two chairs from the corner, offering one to Idris.

"Well, this is rather cosy, isn't it?" Pixley lit a cigarette and leaned back in his chair.

Cardoso's eyes narrowed. "My patience is running thin, Mr Hayford. We placed you and the other guests in protective custody until we can sort out this business. I'm not taking any further risks. A stick of dynamite is beyond even my tolerance level."

Fina surveyed Ruby. Her hands lay folded in her lap as she stared serenely at Cardoso.

"Mr Maghur, special agent from Tripoli—"

Fina's choking noise interrupted Cardoso's explanation.

"Shall I fetch you some water?" asked Idris.

Fina shook her head but looked at Idris in disbelief. He patted her hand.

"Special agent?" Gayatri and Pixley said in unison.

Ruby glared at the pair and they fell silent.

Apparently distracted by the events of the past few hours, Cardoso appeared oblivious to the communication signals flying about the room. "Yes, he confirmed that the person who lodged the crate of wine in front of our tram, and also tied the stick of dynamite to the cat, was none other than M."

"M?" asked Pixley. "Is that who I think it is?"

Idris stopped folding and unfolding a piece of paper and

looked up. "Yes, it is. And we've all had a lucky escape – especially Ruby and Fina."

Gayatri tugged at her plait. "Please be explicit. I haven't been travelling with these three for the past few months, so I don't understand what you're talking about."

Ruby smiled at Gayatri. Gayatri returned the gesture with a devious grin.

Head bent down, Cardoso replied, "M is an international thief, provocateur, master of disguise, and as crooked as a dog's hind leg. We believe she – or he – followed Miss Aubrey-Havelock and Miss Dove to Estoril. We believe M knew the pair were walking into this smuggler's ring and tried to warn them off – by threatening Miss Aubrey-Havelock, in particular."

Fina's face turned hot. "Then you know about the melon and the warning note."

Cardoso nodded.

"Is M part of the smugglers' ring?" asked Gayatri.

"Not directly, though we believe many of the guests are familiar with the existence of M, even if they wouldn't recognise her. We surmise that M benefits from the smugglers' ring and didn't want it to be disturbed."

"And the murder of the Vogels might expose the smugglers' ring if one member committed the murder – and was discovered," said Ruby.

"Precisely." Idris waved his folded piece of paper in Ruby's direction.

Pixley pushed his spectacles further up his nose with one finger. "It's the stuff of novels, but by Jove, it makes sense." He paused. "Except for one thing."

"What might that be?" asked Ruby.

"Well, in addition to the most important question – who killed the Vogels – why wouldn't M just kill Ruby and Fina?"

Gayatri knocked on the wooden table. Fina shivered. Ruby glared.

Pixley held up his hands in mock surrender. "Sorry! But it must be on your minds."

Idris sighed. "I've been worried about that ever since you all arrived in Estoril and I realised M was about. That's why I've stayed in the shadows – I've been watching for signs of M."

"And I'm grateful to you for that," said Cardoso. "Otherwise, we could have all gone up in smoke this afternoon."

"So why try to kill us all then, rather than before?" asked Gayatri.

"Because I was about to reveal the murderers," said Ruby.

Pixley whipped off his spectacles.

"Murderers? As in, more than one villain?"

41

───────────

"Yes, you heard me." Ruby leapt up and paced in a tiny circle behind her chair. "There were two murderers."

"Luckily, everyone in protective custody, so it's simple to extend their stay." A radiant smile spread across Cardoso's face.

"Well, you'll be able to do that with one of them. Perhaps."

"Oh, Ruby Dove, you are a maddening one. I cannot take the suspense any longer!" cried Pixley.

"You should become a barrister," said Gayatri with a tinge of sarcasm.

"Very well, my learned friend," said Ruby, smiling at Gayatri. "Let us begin with Hendrik's murder. What do we know?"

Pixley pulled out his journalist's notebook and flipped through the pages. "He was killed by cyanide. Supposedly a suicide, but we doubt that very much. The police thought the cyanide was on a roulette chip, since he had a habit of biting them for good luck. Only someone who knew him could poison him – which turned out to be everyone around the table. At least, they all knew about his gambling habits as they had seen them before."

"But didn't the police find traces of cyanide in his drink as well?" said Gayatri.

"They did," said Fina, "but we all assumed he'd contaminated the cocktail by taking a drink right after biting the chip. However..." She paused and looked at Ruby.

Ruby stopped pacing and leaned on her chair. "However, what if it was the other way around? What if the cyanide was in his glass first, and it contaminated the chip?"

"Impossible," said the inspector. "He had the glass with him the whole time. There was no chance for it to be poisoned. But Hendrik's chips, they were left unattended."

"Not quite," said Ruby with a smile. "It must have been a ruse – on top of the suicide ruse. Why would someone want us to believe the poison was on the chip and not in his glass?"

They all leaned forward.

"I'll tell you why. Because there was only one person who might have slipped the cyanide into his glass without being seen – besides the bartender himself."

Gayatri hiccupped. "Elke Vogel!"

Ruby nodded. "Precisely. The first thing that tipped me off was her odd behaviour after Hendrik died. Grief takes people in different ways, but it seemed peculiar that she acted as if nothing had happened. That fact forced me to reconsider the poisoning itself. And then I concluded there was only one effective way to administer the poison."

"So she did it in the bar, not at the roulette table at all!" said Gayatri, shaking her head. "And then made sure she wasn't in the room when he got his casino chips, putting herself out of the running as a suspect. How devious."

"It would also make faking the suicide note relatively simple." Pixley doodled on his sketchpad.

"But why?" asked Idris. "Why did Elke kill him?"

Ruby smoothed her hair and pursed her lips. "This is where

it becomes unclear, because we cannot ask either of them to confirm the story. There are a few clues, however, we can piece together. The first is that they were not married."

"How do you know?" asked Gayatri.

Ruby looked to Cardoso. "It's true, isn't it?"

"They were not married, no. We wired to the Dutch authorities and they confirmed it. Miss Dove has guessed correctly yet again." He tipped his espresso cup in her direction.

Pixley looked up from his sketch of a cup of coffee. "So they weren't married, and worked together. That still doesn't give her a reason to kill him."

Fina stared at Pixley's piping hot cup of coffee. It reminded her of cocoa. Chocolate. "This has something to do with their import-export chocolate business, correct?"

Ruby smiled. "Absolutely, Feens. They were definitely a central part of the smuggling ring. Their business allowed them to travel and make deals in ways that others, such as the Princess, could not. That much seemed obvious. But then I began to wonder about Elke. She'd been travelling to places like Berlin and Rome. That didn't fit the pattern. And even for a criminal, it's no easy matter to obtain both an American and a Soviet passport, on top of your national one."

"She had multiple passports?" asked Gayatri.

"We saw them slip out of her handbag when we were in a clothing shop in Estoril. And as for the places they had flown, Jeremy told us about that," replied Fina.

Cardoso held up a thin finger, as if he was pleased to finally have something to contribute to the conversation. "I can confirm Elke Vogel is not her name. She went under at least a dozen different names. Though she worked publicly as a photographer, she must also have been some sort of government agent."

"So she is involved in high-level espionage if she's travelling between Germany and Italy with American and Soviet passports," said Gayatri.

"Her most common aliases were German," said Cardoso. "So it is plausible she was a German agent."

Ruby tapped her teeth. "Yes. It's certainly plausible. I surmise Hendrik must have overheard Elke talking to another agent and realised who she really was. Fina, do you remember that quarrel we overheard between them when they first came into the bar? Hendrik accused her of seeing another man, and I assumed it was your standard, run-of-the-mill love triangle. In fact, she was betraying him in quite a different way. A much more serious way. Elke came to the conclusion that she must be the one to act first. Who knows? She might have been afraid not only of being exposed as an agent, but that he would try to hurt or kill her. That's the reason for such drastic action."

"Where do her photography skills fit into all of this?" asked Fina. "It seems significant."

"Yes, I believe she used photographs for various kinds of threats and extortion – most likely among everyone she worked with. That alone made her a threat."

"So you're saying her death is unrelated to the murder of Hendrik?" asked Gayatri. "My head is swimming!"

"No, the two are linked. Elke's murderer saw an opportunity after Elke killed Hendrik. It's ironic Elke sealed her own fate when she killed Hendrik."

Pixley drummed his fingers on the table. "I say ... you mean she created the opportunity for her own death?"

Gayatri shivered. "But where does Moriarty fit in? You said Moriarty didn't commit the crimes."

"Exactly. Moriarty didn't commit the murder – she wanted to ensure the smuggling ring would continue. Elke's murderer posed a threat to the smuggling ring itself because it gave the police a reason to investigate. Moriarty – and the others – would be worried about discovery."

"That would explain some of their extraordinary behaviour." Idris' voice lowered. "Such as trying to scare you in an aeroplane."

A rush of adrenaline filled Fina's body at the memory of their near crash. "So you're saying Jeremy is the murderer? He tried to scare us?"

Ruby shook her head. "No, Jeremy was just following orders. No doubt he'd been told to go to some lengths to avoid awkward questions. That's what made this case so dashed difficult. The threat of Moriarty looming in the background was enough for everyone to threaten us. Including Florence. That's why she accused me and Lena supported her."

Pixley let out a low whistle.

"As of yesterday, I'd decided that there was only one person could have murdered Elke: the ringleader of the gang. The Princess."

42

The buzzing fly had found a few friends and were now having a smashing party on the windowpane. Fina had to intervene, if only to stop the irritating sound that filled the shocked silence in the room.

"You're saying the Princess committed the murder?"

Ruby smiled. "Sorry. I misled you a bit. Notice I said I *had* decided it was her. That's because she's the ringleader. She had to be, given her connections and the fact she controlled Florence and Lena, not the other way around. She pretended to be weak, ill, and periodically delirious. As weak as an ailing chick. But she was always in control. Who else would have the necessary connections to create an international ring?"

"But why? Why go to all of the trouble? Surely she already lived in great splendour," asked Cardoso.

"I believe it has something to do with her husband's interminable affairs and generally abominable behaviour. She must have been hoarding precious stones for the day when she would escape. Or help organise a *coup d'état*."

Pixley tapped his notebook on the table. "To review. Moriarty put pressure on the members of the smuggling ring to threaten and scare us so we'd leave Estoril."

"Correct."

"And the person with the most to lose was the Princess."

"Correct."

"But you're saying she did not commit the crime."

"No. She did not have the opportunity. Remember, Florence and Teodoro were watching her. In fact, that's why she wanted to join the treasure hunt in the first place. She didn't trust either of them and wanted to watch them."

"Speaking of Teodoro and Florence," said Fina, "did those two have a relationship? They were acting in a peculiar way."

Ruby shook her head. "I suspect something was going on there, but my guess is it was Teodoro trying to remain on good terms with Florence so he could keep his position."

Idris propped his chin up on one hand. "Could the Princess have commanded someone else to do it?"

"But who could she trust to do it? Not Florence, and certainly not Lena."

"What about Teodoro?" asked Gayatri.

"Yes. I thought about Teodoro a great deal. After all, as her guard, he should have done whatever it took to protect her."

"But we know he's working through her to persuade her of his own cause."

"If he is Romanian, however, even if he is Roma, why does he use Hungarian phrases?"

Pixley's mouth hung open. "When did that happen? And how do you know Hungarian?"

"I don't know Hungarian," said Ruby. "But when we were near death in the aeroplane, Lena said, '*Dumnezeule*, my God.' Then, when that unfortunate cat dragged in the dynamite, Teodoro said, '*Istenem*, my God.' I already had my suspicions of him, but this confirmed it. I asked Lena about it and she confirmed that it was Hungarian, not Romanian."

"Couldn't Lena have been lying?" asked Gayatri.

"I doubt it. Why would she be speaking in Hungarian? She's a well-known figure in Romania."

Gayatri covered her face with her hands. "You mean we were tricked? We thought we were seeing a particular operation when it was all fake?"

Ruby shook her head. "I don't think what you saw in that house was fake. But Teodoro must have realised his mistake when he uttered 'please' in Hungarian the night Hendrik was killed. When he said it at the time, I thought it didn't sound Portuguese. It wasn't until I heard the discrepancy between the phrase *my God* that I also asked Lena about how to say 'please' in Romanian." She paused. "I think he realised he let a few words slip in Hungarian around the guests and was worried his plans might be exposed."

"You're saying he knew we were following him, Salvador and Fausto from the beginning?" asked Pixley.

"He counted on it."

"And then when he kidnapped us, it was to convince us his cause was for the Roma when it was really for Hungarians?"

"Yes. In 1919, Romania took Transylvania. Teodoro is Transylvanian. They are planning a coup. Much more serious than persuading the Princess."

"And Elke knew and threatened to expose him."

"She had photographs."

"What photographs?" asked Cardoso.

"In addition to the passports that fell out of her bag, we saw a photograph with a man standing with his back to the camera. A flag hung on the wall," said Ruby. "I asked Lena about the Romanian national flag. Both the Romanian and Transylvanian flags are blue, red, and yellow. The difference is that the Transylvanian has those colours displayed horizontally, while Romania has them vertically."

"But photos are black and white!" cried Cardoso.

Ruby coughed. "Yes, I forgot to tell you that the flag also had a crest with an eagle, castles, moon, and a sun. I also confirmed that with Lena, though she was puzzled by my questions."

Cardoso clicked his tongue and sighed.

"What is it?" asked Ruby.

Cardoso rose and buttoned his jacket. "Teodoro Rapozo said he needed to secure a few items from the hotel for the Princess. An officer is driving him to the hotel as we speak, but I'm concerned Rapozo will do whatever it takes to escape. I must go."

THE CANDLELIGHT FLICKERED as the singer swept past their table, followed by a man with a guitar.

Fina, Gayatri, Idris, Pixley, and Ruby clinked their tumblers of wine. "*Saude!*"

"To our meeting again." Idris lifted his glass higher.

"To another successful conclusion to a case." Pixley lifted his glass to Ruby.

"To us living to see the day." Gayatri moved her glass around the circle, looking each of them in the eye.

Fina bathed in the glow of the wine and candlelight. All around her, people chattered, a cat meowed, and a child wandered in and whined at his mother.

Pixley lit a cigarette. "Remind me, Idris, why we can wander around Lisbon – or I should say, Alfama – without a worry that Moriarty will attack us?"

Idris twisted his tumbler on the table. "After we had that incident in the cafe with the cat and the dynamite, I was fortunate enough to be at the scene. I had been following you in a taxi. When you entered the cafe, I knew Moriarty would still try to attack you, so I hid in the back and waited."

Pixley's eyes lit up. "Did you punch Moriarty?"

"Forgive him," said Gayatri. "Despite his gentle manner, he's positively morbid sometimes. It hits him like a fever."

Idris chuckled and leaned back in his chair. "No, I simply handed Moriarty a note. And I made sure I had on a disguise."

"And the note said..." Fina waved a hand.

"The note said, dear Fina, that I knew all about Moriarty's escapades in Lisbon, and that it would be wise to leave immediately. I included details of various crimes and threats carried out against you and the guests at the hotel and said that I had already alerted the police. Moriarty will not be bothering us for a while."

"What details did you include? I have so many questions!" said Gayatri as she sipped her wine.

Idris spread out his hands.

Gayatri set down her glass. "My first question is why Ruby found a diamond in a clock."

Ruby held up a finger. "I can answer that one – Makeda is responsible. At least, that's my best guess, given her particular pattern of theft. Because she's worried about her mother, she might have stolen the diamond from one of Iveta's clients. Perhaps she was worried that either her mother would find it or that someone else might, in a search of her things when they were looking for other jewels."

"And why did Fina end up with it?" asked Gayatri.

"When I received the note from Idris telling me to go along with being arrested, I gave Fina a hug and slipped the diamond into her pocket so that I couldn't be actually charged with theft."

"So what else did Moriarty do?" asked Pixley. "Did she follow us in the car that first day? Did she steal the dossier from Gayatri's room?"

Idris nodded. "I suspect so. She saw opportunities in both cases."

Fina reached into her bag and pulled out a crumpled slip of paper. She handed it to Idris. "What is the significance of the trapezoid? Why is it on these threatening notes that I assume are from Moriarty?"

Idris rubbed his chin. "As someone who enjoys history, I spent some time researching this. It turns out that some scholars of the Bible say the trapezoid is associated with Satan. Perhaps it's Moriarty's signature."

They sat in silence for a moment.

Pixley's chair rocked back to the ground. "But what about those threats to the Princess? She received letters, and Ruby and Fina witnessed a threat against her life when they were at those shops in Estoril."

"It's possible that Moriarty was threatening her," interjected Ruby, "but it seems more likely that she manufactured the threats herself. She may have even sent a note to a messenger, who notified Paulo that day of the danger. Remember, she had to do everything she could to make it seem that she was the victim."

"There's one more missing piece to this puzzle," said Ruby. "And I cannot figure it out."

Fina, Gayatri, and Pixley goggled at her.

She smiled back at them. "How did Cardoso learn of our previous cases?"

Idris coughed. "I was curious about that as well. I asked Cardoso. At first, he was vague. The reason he was vague, however, was because he was embarrassed that he didn't verify the information source. He received a wire from an officer in London, but didn't check whether this officer was real or not."

Fina rubbed her temples. "Moriarty again."

"But even so, why would he trust us at all?"

Idris coughed again and smiled. "I'm afraid I had a hand in that. Once I found out he knew about you – don't ask how – I arranged to have a follow-up wire sent to him. From the same so-called officer. It said that you all had been helpful in the past."

The guitarist warmed up, strumming softly.

Pixley leaned back in his chair, propping himself up with a foot against the table. "It's rather peculiar, that."

"What? Spill the beans," said Gayatri.

"Have you noticed that Moriarty's schemes have all back-fired? Nothing has worked!"

Gayatri squared her shoulders. "We are rather a formidable team, aren't we, though?"

"Yes, but for an international thief to fail that many times?"

Ruby smiled. "I've had the same thought, Pix. No matter how much I want to flatter ourselves, it does rather feel like a cat playing with a mouse before..." She trailed off. Then she rallied. "But it is five against one, so I suppose we have that in our favour."

Idris leaned forward. "But let's forget that for now and enjoy the music."

The *fado* singer, a beautiful large woman covered in tattoos, moved into position and greeted them in Portuguese. Her guitarist nodded, removed his hat, took a swig from a bottle of water and began to play.

Fina shivered. Tears welled up at the staggering, sweet melancholy of the music.

Under the table, Idris patted her hand and squeezed it.

A child tapped her on the shoulder and handed her a note.

Fina grasped it, wishing it would vanish. Fighting the urge to tear it into confetti, she opened it and read:

Dearest Ruby and Fina,
You may have won this battle, but you certainly have not won the war. I shall return.
Forever yours,
M.

The End

If you enjoyed this book, would you leave a review on your favorite platform? It means a great deal to me. Thank you!

With gratitude,
Rose

MORE RUBY & FINA!

I'm looking to you, dear reader, to share your views about this series. Reviews online are wonderful and word of mouth is even better.

If you enjoyed this book, I would be grateful if you spent a few minutes leaving me a review on your favorite reading platform.

The Ruby Dove Mystery Series:
The Mystery of Ruby's Sugar
The Mystery of Ruby's Port
The Mystery of Ruby's Smoke
Box Set: Mysteries 1-3
Box Set: Mysteries 4-6
The Mystery of Ruby's Stiletto
The Mystery of Ruby's Tracks
The Mystery of Ruby's Mistletoe
The Mystery of Ruby's Roulette

Thank you!

ABOUT THE AUTHOR

Rose Donovan is a lifelong devotee of cozy mysteries. *The Ruby Dove Mystery Series* is her first foray into fiction, though she has written numerous non-fiction articles unraveling the mysteries of politics and injustice.

www.rosedonovan.com
rose@rosedonovan.com
Reader Group
Follow me on Bookbub

NOTE ABOUT BRITISH STYLE

Readers fluent in US English may believe words such as "fuelled", "signalled", "hiccough", "fulfil", titbit", "oesophagus", "blinkers", and "practise" are typographical errors in this text. Rest assured this is simply British spelling. There are also other formatting differences in terms of spacing and punctuation, including periods after quotation marks in certain circumstances.

For Carrie